# THE SIX

Bob was simply a
Who was speakin
him?

Then he saw a dim light somewhere down below. He bent down and saw that he was near some stone steps that led underground. He felt excited. What was all this? Had he discovered some secret hiding-place?

He came in view of the cellar, and stared in astonishment. Four boys sat in the candle-lighted cellar. Bob stood and stared: it looked so cosy and exciting and most surprising to him.

## Also in Beaver
## by Enid Blyton

*The Enchanted Wood*
*The Magic Faraway Tree*
*The Wishing-Chair Again*
*Naughty Amelia Jane!*
*Amelia Jane Again!*
*Amelia Jane is Naughty Again*
*Amelia Jane Gets into Trouble*
*The Children of Cherry-Tree Farm*
*The Children of Willow Farm*
*Come to the Circus*
*Mr Galliano's Circus*
*Circus Days Again*
*Hurrah for the Circus*
*Adventure of the Strange Ruby*
*The Naughtiest Girl in the School*
*The Naughtiest Girl is a Monitor*
*The Adventurous Four*
*The Adventurous Four Again*
*The Adventures of Mr Pink-Whistle*
*Bimbo and Topsy*
*Mr Meddle's Mischief*
*Mr Meddle's Muddles*
*Up The Faraway Tree*
*Welcome, Josie, Click and Bun!*
*The Further Adventures of Josie, Click and Bun*
*Well, Really, Mr Twiddle!*
*Hello, Mr Twiddle!*
*The Boy Who Wanted a Dog*
*The Birthday Kitten*
*The Very Big Secret*
*Hollow Tree House*
*House At The Corner*

# THE SIX
# BAD BOYS

*Enid Blyton*

*Illustrated by Bob Harvey*

Beaver Books

*This book is dedicated*
*with respect and affection*
*to*
BASIL HENRIQUES, C.B.E., J.P.
Chairman of the East London Juvenile Court
*without whose inspiration*
*this story could not*
*have been written*

A Beaver Book
Published by Arrow Books Limited
62–5 Chandos Place, London WC2N 4NW

An imprint of Century Hutchinson Ltd

London Melbourne Sydney Auckland
Johannesburg and agencies throughout the world

First published by Lutterworth Press 1951

Beaver edition 1987

Text © Darrell Waters 1951
Illustrations © Century Hutchinson Ltd 1987
Enid Blyton is the Registered Trade Mark
of Darrell Waters Limited

Set in Times
by JH Graphics Ltd, Reading

Made and printed in Great Britain
by Anchor Brendon Ltd
Tiptree, Essex

ISBN 0 09 947240 6

# Contents

## A Note for the Reader
## from the Author

Are you a child? Or are you a grown-up? It doesn't much matter, with this book. It is written for the whole family, and for anyone who has to do with children. It is written, as all stories are written, to entertain the reader — but it is written too to explain some of the wrong things there are in the world, and to help to put them right.

I love children, good or bad. I know plenty of good ones — and I have been to the Juvenile Courts and seen plenty of bad ones. One of the finest magistrates of these Courts is the well-known Mr Basil Henriques, who deals so wisely and kindly with all the delinquent children brought before him. I have watched him at his Court dealing with these children.

In trepidation, I asked him if he would be kind enough to read through my book to see if I had made any mistakes in Court procedure. I cannot thank him enough for taking so much trouble. I could not have had better advice than his.

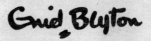

## CHAPTER ONE

# Two Families Move In

Donald and Jeanie ran to the window when they heard the sound of heavy wheels outside. They pulled back the curtain.

'The new people are moving in next door!' said Jeanie. 'The van has come, Mother. I wonder who they are. Will there be children, do you think?'

'I expect so,' said their mother. 'No, Pat, you can't go to the window and look out till you've drunk up your milk. Drink it quickly!'

Pat drank her milk so quickly that she spluttered. Then she ran to the window too. All the Mackenzies watched the big van draw up at the bungalow next door.

Donald and Jeanie were twins, eleven years old. Pat was their seven-year-old sister. They lived in Barlings Cottage with their mother and father, and their dog Frisky.

Frisky was at the front gate, his paws up, his nose through the bars of the gate. He was watching too.

'He's hoping there will be a dog to play with!' said Donald. 'Look – they're opening the van doors.'

'Only the removal men are there,' said Jeanie, disappointed. 'Where are the family?'

'Oh, they'll come by train, I expect,' said their mother, busy clearing away the breakfast. 'They'll be here soon, because someone will have to tell the men where to put the furniture. Jeanie, aren't you going to help clear away for me?'

Jeanie ran to help, trying to be as quick as possible

because she wanted to go back and watch to see what family was coming to Hawthorn Cottage. She did hope there would be children. The last people in the bungalow had been two old ladies and they hadn't liked children at all.

Then Donald gave a yell. 'I say! There's *another* van coming! Surely that little bungalow next door won't hold *two* vans of furniture! Why, even we only had one van when we moved here, and that wasn't a very big one.'

Mrs Mackenzie came to the window herself, puzzled to hear about two vans for such a small cottage. Why, it had only two bedrooms!

'It's not stopping at Hawthorn Cottage,' she said. 'It's going on; it's going to the house on our *other* side – Summerhayes. Those people must be moving in today too.'

Summerhayes was a house, not a bungalow. It was not a very pretty house, but it was bigger than either Barlings or Hawthorn Cottage. The second van came to a standstill outside Summerhayes, and the men at the front got down and went round to the back. At the same moment a small car drew up beside the van.

'This *is* exciting,' said Donald. '*Two* families moving in on the same day, one on each side. What fun if they both have children! We shall have plenty to play games with then.'

'There are five people in the car,' said Jeanie. 'Look, Pat – can you see them? There's a mother – and a father – and are those children at the back?'

The back door of the car swung open and three children scrambled out. The Mackenzie family watched them eagerly.

There were two girls about twelve and thirteen, and

8

a boy about ten. The boy pushed past his sisters and ran up the path to the Summerhayes front door.

'I don't much like the look of the boy,' said Donald. 'Hark at him banging at the knocker! He must know the house is empty.'

The mother shouted something crossly at the boy and he swung round and grinned. One of his sisters gave him a sharp push as she came up the path to the door, and he pushed her back.

Then the new family disappeared inside the door, and the removal men swung open the back doors of the van and began to pull out a table.

'Look — two people are going into Hawthorn

Cottage now, on the other side of us!' said Pat. 'Are they the family there, do you think?'

'Yes,' said Jeanie, and all three children looked closely at the good-looking woman with the equally good-looking boy walking up to the front door of the cottage nearby. The woman took out a key and unlocked the door. She and the boy disappeared inside.

'A family of three children one side and one boy on the other side,' said Donald. 'Not bad! We'll be able to make some new friends, anyway. We haven't had children for neighbours all the time we've been here. It'll be nice, won't it, Mother?'

'Yes,' said his mother, bustling round. 'Jeanie, I shall want you to call in at both houses some time soon and offer to take them pots of tea – just to be neighbourly when they're all in a muddle.'

'I'll go with her,' said Donald, who was longing to get a closer look at the four new children.

'So will I,' said Pat.

'No. Three will be too many,' said Jeanie at once. Pat said no more, but her mother saw she was disappointed. Pat was so often left out by the twins, who were everything to each other.

'Poor little odd-man-out!' thought Mrs Mackenzie for the hundredth time. 'She's always on her own. I hope one of these four children will make friends with her – perhaps the only boy next door, at Hawthorns.'

A great bustle went on all the morning. The removal men carried the furniture into the houses, and staggered under an enormous wardrobe for Summerhayes, and a piano for Hawthorns. They took in tables and chairs and sofas and pictures, a washing machine for Summerhayes, and an ordinary wash-tub for the bungalow.

'It'll be funny to see all that furniture set out neatly

in the rooms!' said Jeanie. 'Mother, is it time for me to go and offer the new people tea?'

'Yes. It's past eleven,' said her mother. 'Just say that Mrs Mackenzie next door would be pleased to send in a pot of tea, because they must be feeling the need of something!'

Jeanie and Donald set off. Pat watched them go. 'Would *you* like to go and ask at Hawthorns next door if they would like some tea?' said Mrs Mackenzie to Pat.

'Oh *no!*' said Pat, at once. 'I'd be much too scared to go to people I didn't know. I wouldn't have minded going with Donald and Jeanie. But they never want me.'

'Oh yes they do,' said her mother. 'It's just that they're twins, and twins are always like that. They wouldn't be without you for the whole world!'

'I wish I'd been a twin too,' said Pat. 'Look Mother – they've gone right inside Summerhayes!'

Donald and Jeanie had walked up to the front door, and had rung the bell politely. But nobody had answered. There was a great deal of noise going on upstairs, as if furniture was being shifted round and about. A girl's voice called something, and then there was the sound of furniture being dragged across the floor again.

'They'll never hear us ringing the bell,' said Donald, peering into the hall. 'Look, they've got the carpets down already. Let's go in and find the people and give them Mother's message.'

They went into the hall. They heard voices in the kitchen and decided to go there. But outside the kitchen door they stopped.

A woman's voice was raised in anger. 'You said you would arrange about having the gas laid on ready – and it isn't! And there's no lino down here, either. What's the good of you, I'd like to know? Here I've been slaving away for the past two weeks, packing

11

and getting ready, and making new curtains – and leaving just a *few* things to you. And as usual they're not done!'

The voice was sharp and harsh. Donald and Jeanie moved back quickly into the hall. 'Was that the mother?' said Jeanie. 'Who was she talking to? One of the removal men?'

'I don't know,' said Donald. 'What a horrid voice! Shall we go upstairs and find someone else?'

But before they could decide what to do the kitchen door swung open and two people came out, a man and a woman. The woman looked angry, and the man looked sullen. They stopped in surprise when they saw Jeanie and Donald.

'Please excuse us for coming in,' said Donald hastily, 'but we live next door – and our mother sent us in to say she would be glad to send in a pot of tea if you'd like it. She knows what a muddle moving in is.'

'Well, that's kind of her,' began the man, but the woman interrupted him.

'Please thank your mother,' she said, stiffly, 'but tell her we won't trouble her for the tea. We can easily boil a kettle on the gas stove. You're the children next door, you say?'

'Yes,' said Donald. 'We're twins. We live at Barlings.'

There was a clatter on the stairs and three children came down at top speed. 'Mother, where's my little chair? It hasn't been left behind, has it?' shouted one of the girls.

Then they saw Jeanie and Donald and stared at them curiously. 'These are the children from next door,' said their mother. She turned to Jeanie and Donald. 'Well, you run along home,' she said. 'And give your mother my thanks.'

'Here, what are your names?' said the boy, as they

turned to go. His mother frowned at him and waved him back. The twins heard quite well what she said, though her voice was low.

'We don't know what the family is like yet. I may not want you to know them.'

The twins were scarlet with fury when they got to the gate. 'Horrid woman!' said Jeanie. 'And she told a lie too. She said she would boil a kettle on the gas stove – and we heard her telling her husband there wasn't any gas! I don't like her one bit.'

'I didn't like the boy much either,' said Donald, cross and disappointed. 'Let's go and tell Mother.'

They ran into their own front gate, and soon Mrs Mackenzie heard of their experience next door. She laughed at their furious faces.

'Don't be so cross! They're probably all hot and bothered with moving in, and may think we're poking our noses in too soon.'

'I don't want to go and ask at Hawthorns if they would like tea,' said Jeanie. 'They might be just as rude!'

'You won't need to,' said her mother. 'Here comes the next-door boy himself!'

CHAPTER TWO

## Making Friends

A very good-looking boy was walking up the front path. He was dressed in jersey and shorts, and his dark curly hair was thick and unruly. He had bright, cheeky eyes and a smile that won Pat's heart at once.

'Good morning,' he said to Mrs Mackenzie when she came to the door. 'I expect you've seen us moving in next door – my Mum and I. Mum says she hates to bother you, but could you possibly lend us a kettle to make a pot of tea? Our kettle has completely disappeared.'

'Well, I was just going to send in to ask if you'd like a pot,' said Mrs Mackenzie. 'I'll lend you a kettle too, with pleasure. Come in and wait a minute and I'll make you some tea and you can take it back with you.'

The boy came in. He grinned at the twins and Pat. 'Hallo! You're neighbours, aren't you? Does anything exciting go on in this town? I lived in Croydon before, and my word there was always something going on there. I belonged to a fine gang.'

'What's a gang?' asked Pat.

'Oh – a whole lot of boys – and girls too sometimes,' said the boy. 'What's your name? Mine's Bob Kent.'

'We're twins, Jeanie and Donald, and this is Pat. She's only a baby – she's seven. We're eleven,' said Jeanie.

'She's no baby!' said Bob, grinning at Pat. 'I once had a seven-year-old cousin to stay with me, and she was up to all sorts of tricks. I bet Pat is too.'

Pat was delighted at this. She never did get up to tricks, but she didn't mind this boy thinking she did. She smiled broadly at him, hoping that he would be friends with her, and not with Jeanie and Donald. But he was so big for his age – he would never want a little girl like Pat!

Mrs Mackenzie went into the scullery to boil a kettle. She liked Bob too – a merry boy with plenty of go in him, she thought. It would be fun for her family to have him to play with.

'Is your father coming soon?' asked Jeanie. 'We only saw your mother.'

'My father's dead,' said Bob. 'He died last year. I miss him an awful lot. There's only Mum and me, so I like to look after things – when she'll let me!'

The twins felt sorry about Bob's father. They loved their own father very much – he was cheerful and loving, and also strict, but they didn't mind that so long as he loved them! They thought it must be dreadful not to have a father to say 'Yes, you may' or 'No, certainly not!' or to take them to the Zoo or on a picnic with Mother.

Mrs Mackenzie appeared with the tea. She had put it on a tray with a jug of milk. She had put a glass of lemonade on the tray as well, and a plate of biscuits.

'Oh, thanks awfully,' said Bob. 'I shall love a drink of lemonade. I'll bring back the tray later. And thanks for the kettle too.'

He went off, carrying the tray carefully, giving Pat a broad wink as he went. She didn't like to wink back. She stared after him, thinking that it really would be fun to have him next door. He didn't think her a baby, so he might quite well play with her.

'Did you like Bob, Mother?' asked Donald. 'I did. He'll be fun – up to all kinds of things.'

'Yes, I liked him,' said Mrs Mackenzie, secretly wondering what kind of things Bob would be 'up to'. He had a bold look about him – she thought he would dare to do a good many things he ought not to do. And what a good-looking boy he was!

She looked at the twins – red haired and freckled with greeny-brown eyes. Pat wasn't red-haired, she was dark with brown eyes. Mrs Mackenzie hoped that Bob would take a little notice of Pat. Pat was too shy, and too dreamy, and she suffered because the others were twins and didn't need her. That made her a bit of a 'mother's girl', but it couldn't very well be helped.

Frisky the dog ran in, wagging his tail. He had taken the boy right to his front door. He liked him. He liked his loud, cheerful voice, and the way he stroked him and patted him – firmly, and confidently. Frisky thought he was the right kind of boy for a dog!

'Well, anyway we've got *one* nice neighbour,' said Donald. 'I expect he'll go to school with us.'

It was Saturday, so there was no school that day. The twins went off for a walk with Frisky in the afternoon, and Pat went with her mother to see her aunt, though she wished and wished she could go with Jeanie and Donald.

The two new families settled in that day and the next. Curtains went up, and the houses began to look lived-in. When lights shone from the window at night the Mackenzies felt pleased.

'It's nice to have people living each side of us again,' said Jeanie. 'Mother, may we ask Bob to tea some time?'

'Ask him for Thursday,' said Mother. 'Then he will have had time to settle in.'

Bob appeared in their school on the Tuesday. He was in a class below Jeanie and Donald, but higher than Pat's, of course. The other three children from Summerhayes appeared also. They were well-dressed and neat.

They gave their names as Eleanor, Hilda, and Thomas Berkeley. Bob gave his as Robert Kent. He rushed up to Jeanie and Donald when the eleven o'clock break came.

'Hallo! I went to call for you this morning but you'd gone. Hallo, Pat! Have one of my biscuits?'

'Oh, thank you,' said Pat, proud that the big boy had singled her out for a biscuit.

'Are those the kids from the house on the other side of you?' asked Bob, nodding towards Eleanor, Hilda, and Thomas. 'They look pretty stuck-up – and the boy looks bad-tempered, I think.'

'He's not very nice to his sisters,' said Jeanie. 'I saw him push one over just now.'

'Well, *I* might push a sister over if she was stuck-up,' said Bob. 'Come on – let's play burglars and policemen. I'll be the burglar, you be the policemen. And Pat can be a detective and watch all I do.'

Bob made it a most exciting game, and they were all sorry when the bell went for lessons again. Bob shoved past Thomas as they went in. Thomas shoved back at once.

'Here! Who are you shoving?' he said.

'You,' said Bob, cheerfully. 'What are you called – Thomas or Tom? I'm Bob. I live two doors away from you.'

'I'm Tom Berkeley,' said Tom, and looked closely at Bob. Bob grinned back, and Tom gave a sudden grin too, which made his sulky face look quite different.

The Mackenzies, Bob and Tom all walked home together. Eleanor and Hilda walked some way behind, talking in low voices. They had been polite but not friendly.

'Haven't made up their minds yet whether they want to know us or not!' Jeanie said to Donald.

Frisky came rushing to meet the children. Bob made a great fuss of him and so did Tom. 'I wish I had a dog,' said Tom. 'I've always wanted one, but my mother said it would have to belong to all of us if we had one, and I want a dog of my own.'

'But Frisky belongs to all of *us*!' said Donald. 'We all share him – and he likes it.'

'You wouldn't like sharing anything with *my* two sisters,' said Tom.

'I'd like a dog too,' said Bob. 'But my mother says

they're a nuisance. They bring in mud and all that.'

'But you can always clear it up,' said Jeanie. 'What's it matter? Donald and I always clear up any mud Frisky brings in.'

'And I pick off the hairs he leaves on Mother's sofa,' said Pat. 'I'm glad *our* mother likes dogs.'

'Oh, my mother lets me have anything else I like,' said Bob, at once. 'I go to the cinema, and I get plenty of sweets, and I've got a fine railway set. The rails take up the whole floor when they're set out.'

'I had a set like that too,' said Tom. 'But when we moved out of our big house to this small house, my mother sold my railway set. She said there wouldn't be room to play with it here. My father was angry, because he'd said I *could* keep it. There was a fine old row.'

Jeanie and Donald remembered the loud, harsh voice scolding in the kitchen of the house next door, when the Berkeleys had moved in. They didn't somehow think they would like Tom's mother – especially if she had sold his lovely railway set!

'Will your father buy you another one?' asked Pat.

'No. Mother would only sell that too,' said Tom. 'Do you know what he said? He said that he would sell one of my mother's brooches because she'd sold my railway set! So she locks all her jewellery away. When she sold my railway set I'd a good mind to take one of her brooches myself and sell it!'

All the others looked at him, shocked and disbelieving. What a dreadful thing to say!

'Don't you love your mother?' said Pat, in an amazed voice. 'You couldn't do a thing like that to her!'

Tom looked suddenly ashamed. He began to whistle loudly, then he stopped. 'Look at old Frisky!' he said, changing the subject very abruptly indeed. 'He's found a bone or something!'

Frisky had indeed found a bone – but unfortunately it belonged to another dog! The dog leapt at him, growling, and Frisky dodged aside, still holding on to the bone. The other dog leapt again.

'Oh – Frisky will be bitten!' cried Pat. 'He won't let go the bone!'

Bob ran to the two growling dogs, and caught Frisky by the tail. Frisky barked crossly – and dropped the bone! The other dog snapped it up and was off at once.

'Good work!' said Tom admiringly to Bob. 'I say – that was jolly plucky of you. You might have been badly bitten. I hate to interfere when two dogs begin a fight.'

'Thank you, Bob!' said Jeanie, and she thumped him on the back. 'Frisky, you're bad to steal another dog's bone. Bad dog!'

Tom seemed to be very struck with Bob's action. 'I wouldn't have done that for worlds,' he said. 'I say, let me come and see your railway some time, will you?'

Bob was pleased. He liked being praised by a bigger boy. 'I'll ask my mother when you can come,' he said. 'Well, here we all are – I'm off to my dinner. Goodbye!'

CHAPTER THREE

## Inside Three Houses

Soon the three families were friendly with one another. Apparently Mrs Berkeley decided that the Mackenzies were nice enough to know, and she smiled and nodded to Mrs Mackenzie when she met her out shopping.

Mrs Kent was also very friendly, and soon the three women had been to tea with one another. Mrs Berkeley's house was nicely furnished, and had some lovely rugs and pictures. Mrs Kent's things were beautifully kept, and she took great pride in her house.

But Mrs Mackenzie really didn't like either of the women next door very much. She shook her head when her husband said he was pleased that she had found friends each side of her.

'Mrs Berkeley is so discontented,' she said. 'They had a big house, and because her husband lost his job, and had to get one not so good, she is very bitter. She thinks he is no good and she told him so.'

'Very disloyal of her, then,' said her husband. 'You'd not say a thing like that about me if I lost my job and we had to move!'

'I could never say a word against you, anyhow, whether you deserved it or not,' said Mrs Mackenzie, darning a stocking quite fiercely. 'And you *don't* deserve it, Andrew. I had half a mind to tell Mrs Berkeley not to talk against her husband behind his back. I will too, one of these days!'

'Maybe she's just letting off steam to you,' said Mr Mackenzie. 'She might not tell anyone else.'

'Oh, but she says things in front of the children!' said Mrs Mackenzie, indignantly. 'What would you say, Andy, I'd like to know, if I told you you were a nitwit in front of the twins and Pat? That's what she said to her husband — in front of me *and* her children!'

'It's bad for the children,' said her husband. 'But maybe she said it in fun, Jessie.'

'That boy is fond of his father,' said his wife, still darning at top speed. 'It's going to be hard for Tom if his mother tries to turn him away from Mr Berkeley. It looks to me as if the girls side with her all the time.'

'Now don't you get yourself all worked up about other people's children,' said Mr Mackenzie. 'We've enough on our hands with ours. What do you think of that other boy — Bob Kent?'

'I like him,' said Mrs Mackenzie. 'But he does need a father! He bosses his mother around — or tries to, because she won't let him! I know why he does it, he thinks he's got to be the man of the house; and he adores his mother, but she wants to rule *him*. She gets tired of his domineering ways, and pushes him off. Poor Bob — he'd be all right in a proper family, like ours. He's as good as gold with little Pat.'

'Yes. He's nice with Pat,' agreed Mr Mackenzie. 'Pat's *our* problem, isn't she? She's all drawn into herself, too shy, too alone — can't say boo to a goose!'

'Yes. The twins make her miserable because they don't want her. They're quite sufficient for each other,' said Mrs Mackenzie, laying down her darning for a minute. 'And it's so natural for twins to be like that, that I can't really blame them! Families *are* difficult, aren't they, Andy?'

She smiled at her husband. He smiled back. 'They are never too difficult to handle if you face the problems, Jess,' he said. 'But we've all got to pull together. Pat will be all right. We all love her and that's what matters — even if she does feel one on her own. But maybe Bob will be good for her. And she'll certainly be good for him! He needs a brother or sister as much as he needs a father.'

'He wants a father like *you*,' said his wife, taking up the stocking again. 'He could do with a spanking now and again. He's a nice boy, but too big for his boots, sometimes. He just wants keeping in order. Like you keep the twins in order!'

Her husband grinned, and began to fill his pipe.

'Poor Donald! He got a whacking last week, didn't he, for borrowing my bicycle without telling me, and putting it back in the shed covered with mud! But he knew he deserved it.'

'Well, you're his father, and if fathers can't keep their boys on the right road it's a poor look-out for the boys!' said his wife. 'Anyway he knew he'd earned the whacking. He won't borrow things without asking again!'

So they talked over their neighbours, and in their turn their neighbours talked over the Mackenzies.

'Not quite our style,' said Mrs Berkeley to her husband. 'We wouldn't know them if we were still living in our other house.'

'Speak for yourself, Amy,' said her husband. 'I like that Scotsman next door. And Mackenzie's a good

fellow, and his wife seems a very nice little woman. I don't like the way you look down on people. I never did.'

'And I don't like the way you find fault with me!' said his wife. 'Who lost his job and brought us down to *this*, I'd like to know! This potty little house, and having to send the children to school with boys like that Bob Kent!'

'I don't see much wrong with Bob Kent either,' said her husband, exasperated. 'He's friendly with Tom and seems a jolly sort of boy. Tom wants a friend. He's only got two sisters, and he's a proper boy; the two girls tease him so, too.'

'Oh, there you go again – it's always Tom that's in the right, and the girls that are in the wrong,' said Mrs Berkeley, her voice rising.

'Don't let's discuss the matter,' said Mr Berkeley wearily, unfolding his newspaper. 'I wish we were like the Mackenzies. I'm pretty certain they don't nag and bicker all the time.'

'Mrs Mackenzie doesn't *need* to nag her husband!' said Mrs Berkeley bitterly. 'He does things without being nagged at. He . . .'

The two girls came into the room. Mr Berkeley frowned at his wife to make her stop. But she went on, raising her voice.

'If you were like Mr Mackenzie and looked after your family properly, and could be trusted, and . . .'

Mr Berkeley got up and went out of the room, an ugly look on his face. His wife burst into tears, and Eleanor and Hilda hurried to her at once.

'Don't cry, Mummy! Is Dad in a bad temper again? Don't cry! It's *horrid* of him to make you cry!'

And that evening neither Eleanor nor Hilda would look at or speak to their father, however hard he tried to break the ice! Tom was puzzled by their sulks, and sorry for his father. He began to tell him about a film he had seen, and his father, only too glad to have some friendliness from one of his family, listened with great attention.

But that, of course, made his mother and sisters angry with Tom, and as soon as Mr Berkely had gone out of the room to answer the telephone, they rounded on him.

'Sucking up to Dad!' said Eleanor, scornfully. 'Always on Dad's side! Just like you, Tom.'

'What do you mean?' said Tom, surprised. 'Oh – has there been a row? Well *I* didn't know! This family is always having silly rows. Why can't I talk to Dad if I want to, anyway? *I* wasn't in the row!'

'You might stick up for poor Mother,' said Hilda.

24

'You know quite well that if it hadn't been for Dad's silliness over his business we wouldn't be here, in this little house, and having to go to school with children like Bob and the Mackenzies.'

'Why, what's wrong with them?' said Tom, exasperated. 'You girls! You're always so catty and stuck-up and idiotic!'

'Oh, Tom – you're getting just like your father!' said his mother, and tears fell down her cheeks again.

Tom couldn't bear to see his mother cry, and she knew it. He looked at her, feeling suddenly miserable. He got up and went to her, but she pushed him away.

'No – you're on your father's side! Don't come round *me*! You don't love me as your sisters do.'

'I'm not on anybody's side,' said Tom, staring miserably at his mother. 'Why can't we all get on together? *I* don't mind this house being little. I think it's nice. And I like the school and the children there – especially the Mackenzies. I don't know why you turn your nose up at them. They're clever and . . .'

'He likes everybody except his own family,' said Eleanor, spitefully. 'He likes those silly Mackenzies more than he likes his own sisters!'

Tom felt his temper rising. He rounded on Eleanor, glaring at her. 'I *don't* like you when you're like this! I hate you! I'm not surprised I like the Mackenzies when my own family behaves like this – all because I talked to Dad, and . . .'

'He said he hates me,' wailed Eleanor, who loved a scene as much as her mother did. Her mother drew her down beside her, patting her shoulder. Tom stared at them both, made a rude face at Hilda, and stalked out of the room. He would go and find Bob. They'd think of something exciting to do together.

Bob had been talking to *his* mother, about the

25

Mackenzies. He liked them all very much, especially Mr Mackenzie. The Scotsman's mixture of kindness and firmness to his family fascinated Bob, who had no father to turn to or to respect.

His mother listened with half an ear. She was bored with this town of Lappington to which she had just come. She missed her old friends. She was bored with Bob's conversation. She was even bored with Bob. How dirty and noisy and stupid young boys were, she thought. And how annoying Bob was when he tried to run the whole place, and lay down the law – trying to be the man of the house!

Bob couldn't very well help trying to be the man of the house. He had a strong, determined nature, and no father to check it. He loved his mother and wanted to look after her, and the last thing his father had told him was to play the man and run things for his mother.

So Bob got in the coal – but expected to go with his mother everytime she went to the cinema. He took her early tea in the morning – but turned on the radio full blast at all hours of the day if he felt like it, and glared when his mother turned it off. He fetched the papers for her – but stayed out as late as he liked at night!

Three families, all living so close together, and all so very different!

CHAPTER FOUR

# *Mostly About Tom*

After five or six weeks the three families felt as if they had known each other for quite a long time, at least, the children did.

They went to the same school at the same times each day. They knew the same teachers, they played the same games. Eleanor and Hilda soon lost their 'stuckupness' when they saw that the other children didn't care whether the Berkeleys thought themselves grand or not. But the two girls still *thought* themselves superior to the others, though they didn't show it very often.

All three boys were friends, but because Jeanie was Donald's twin she went everywhere with them, and they thought of her almost as a boy. Pat was more left out than ever!

But she wasn't as lonely as before, because Bob was very good to her. He often left the others and went in search of her. He would pop his head round the sitting-room door and call her.

'Pat! You *are* a mouse! Come out and have a run with me. We'll go down to the canal and sail a boat.'

Mrs Mackenzie would nod to Pat. 'Yes, go with Bob.' She knew she could trust the boy with Pat, and she saw how happy the little girl was to be with him. She thought it was good of the big boy to take so much notice of such a little girl.

'If I had a sister, Pat, I'd like her to be just like you,' Bob said one day to Pat. She beamed.

'I'd like you for a brother too,' she managed to say.

'But you've got Donald,' Bob said.

'Yes, I know. But he always seems to be Jeanie's brother, not mine,' explained Pat. 'I'd like to have a brother of my own – like Jeanie has Donald.'

'Well, *I'll* be your brother,' said Bob. 'You're one on your own and so am I. If you want anything, you come to me, see?'

Those few words meant all the world to Pat. Here was someone who didn't push her aside as the twins did, although they never meant to be unkind. She began to talk to Bob as she had never talked to anyone before, and he listened gravely and seriously.

But he wasn't grave or serious with the others: he was loud-voiced and bold and daring! It was always he who jumped first over the stream to see if it was too wide for safety. It was always he who climbed the tallest trees, and dropped from the highest walls. He thrilled the class at school by being cheeky to the teachers, he was ready to do anything.

Tom admired him. Tom was a determined boy too, but given to sulks and resentments. Often he would exasperate the others by flaring up unexpectedly, and walking off in a fury.

'*Now* what's the matter with Tom?' Jeanie would say. 'He's so *awkward* today – keeps on spoiling everything. Really, I could slap him!'

'Had a row at home, I expect,' said Bob. And more than likely Bob would be right. The bickering went on all the time, with poor Tom pulled first one way and then the other. It was heaven to him to slip into the Mackenzie's home after a quarrel, and sit and listen to the family talk of the whole Mackenzie family.

'What's up, Tom?' Mr Mackenzie said one evening,

28

when the boy slipped into the room, said a word to Donald, and then sat perfectly silent in a corner.

'Nothing,' said Tom. 'I like this room, that's all.'

Mrs Mackenzie knew that it wasn't the room he liked. It was sitting there in peace, hearing no hard words and no tearful cries. She frowned warningly at her husband to tell him to take no notice of Tom.

'It's Pat's birthday soon,' said Mrs Mackenzie. 'We'll have to have a birthday party for her. Well, well, Pat − to think you'll be eight!'

'I've got a fine surprise for you, Pat,' said Donald. 'I've been making it for weeks.'

'And I've been saving up my money to buy you something you *badly* want!' said Jeanie. 'Frisky's going to give you something too!'

'Wuff wuff,' said Frisky, obligingly, and thumped his tail on the floor.

'That dog understands every word we say,' said Mr Mackenzie, looking up from his paper. 'I remember once I had a dog who used to die for the king . . .'

Frisky at once rolled over and lay perfectly still. Mr Mackenzie went on:

'And he could sit up and beg too . . .'

Frisky leapt up, sat on his haunches and begged, waving his paws in the air.

'And he could even shut the door when somebody left it open,' said Mr Mackenzie, with a grin at Tom, who had left it open when he came in.

And to Tom's enormous surprise Frisky ran to the door, stood himself up and shut it with a click!

'Gosh, isn't he clever!' said Tom. 'I'm sorry I left the door open. But I say − do go on talking and see if Frisky will do all you say. What about telling him that that other dog you knew could turn the radio on! I'd love to see Frisky do that!'

29

Donald and Jeanie roared. 'Idiot, Tom – you don't *really* believe Frisky did all those things for the first time, do you? They're tricks he knows quite well. Daddy was pretending to talk about another dog, knowing that Frisky was listening and would do the things he understood.'

'I once knew a dog who would turn on the radio, Frisky,' said Tom, suddenly. But this was a trick that Frisky *didn't* know, so he merely wagged his tail politely and looked inquiringly up at Tom.

It was very pleasant in the Mackenzies' house. True the twins got into trouble sometimes, and were firmly and immediately punished. They said they were sorry – and then no more was said about the matter at all. Everything was just the same as ever!

'No bickering, no nagging, no quarrelling, no weeping and crying!' Tom often thought to himself. 'When *I* do anything wrong I'm grumbled at for ages, and punished and scolded and reminded of what I've done for days! It's easy, too, for the Mackenzies to be loyal to both their parents – they're not pulled this way and that as I am.'

Poor Tom often brooded over this. If he tried to please his father then his mother would look at him reproachfully. If he did his best to make his mother happy his father would look at him scornfully. Tom thought he had a most uncomfortable family!

No wonder he tried to get away from it so often. No wonder he liked to slip into the Mackenzie's house and listen to their talk. He was not at all surprised when he found his father there one evening, listening-in to a special concert with Mr Mackenzie!

His father spoke to him as they went home together. 'Don't tell your mother I was listening to that concert at the Mackenzies', Tom. She was so cross with me this evening that I knew she would grumble at me all through the concert if I had the radio on at home, and I did want to hear it in peace.'

So when Tom was asked by his mother where he and his father had been, he told an untruth.

'We just went for a walk,' he said looking sulky because he felt uncomfortable.

'Where to?' asked his mother.

'Er – to the canal,' said Tom.

'Whatever for?' asked Eleanor. 'Pouring with rain and you go down to the canal! I bet you weren't there. I bet you were next door with those Mackenzies. You simply live there these days! That's where you were, isn't it?'

'I told you, I was with Dad,' said Tom, desperately. 'Shut up talking at me like that. I want to read.'

'I shall ask Jeanie tomorrow if you *were* at her house,' said Hilda, maliciously. Tom said nothing, but his heart sank. He didn't want the Mackenzies to know that he had lied – but how could he let his father down? Tom was torn in two again! He sat and sulked all the rest of the evening and would hardly say a word even to his father.

It was Dad who had got him into this muddle. Now if Hilda found out they had both been at the Mackenzies' that evening, and not down to the canal, there would be another big row – not only with him, but with his father as well. Tom brooded over it, and felt that he disliked his father too that evening.

But fortunately Hilda forgot all about the matter, and didn't ask the Mackenzies any awkward questions, so Tom breathed more freely.

'I'll be more careful next time I tell a lie,' he thought. 'It's no good telling my family the truth. If I'd said we were listening to the Mackenzies' radio Mother would have raged all evening. I don't blame Dad for popping in there, I like it myself.'

After that Tom often told lies when he wanted to get out of trouble, or if he wanted to do something he thought his mother wouldn't like him to do.

'I'm going to see if Harry's at home,' he would say, knowing that he wasn't going there at all. He was off to the cinema! It was a film he wasn't supposed to see, but he knew a door he could slip in by without getting a ticket. He had found it by accident one evening.

Or he would say he was going off for a walk with one of his school friends when all the time he was hanging round a fun-fair that had set itself up in the town. His father and mother believed him, and off he went. He liked the blare of the cheerful music, and the bright lights of the fair. He liked to watch the people working the automatic machines there. It was better than sitting at home and hearing quarrels!

He met Bob there once. Bob had been out to tea and was coming back. The boys bumped into one another.

'Hallo, Bob!' said Tom. 'Come and look at these machines with me. There's rather a good one with little men that play football. If you win you get your money back.

Bob looked on, fascinated. He had a 10p coin and he produced it. Tom produced one too. They worked the handles feverishly, making the little figures kick at a ball that rolled here and there. At last Tom made one of his side kick a goal.

He got his 10p back. 'Have another game!' he asked Bob.

Bob shook his head. 'No. That was my last 10p. I don't get much pocket-money, you know. Not as much as you do! Come on home.'

'No,' said Tom. 'I'll stay here for a bit.' So Bob left him and went home, wondering what Tom's father would say if he could see Tom down in the fun-fair so late at night.

## CHAPTER FIVE

## Bob and his Mother

Bob's mother wasn't too pleased with him when he came in that night, much later than she had told him to be in.

'I suppose you think you're sixteen!' she said to him. 'Well, you're not. You're not even twelve! And you've got to be in at the time I tell you.'

'But you said *you* were going out to tea, too,' said Bob. 'Why shouldn't I go as well?'

'You'll just do as you're told,' said his mother. 'It's enough bother to have to stay at home and look after you, as it is, without your being disobedient and headstrong.'

Bob looked at her in surprise. '*Am* I a bother?' he asked. 'How am I? I'm at school all day, except for dinner. I can take my dinner to school if you like. Some of the children do. But after all you've got nothing to do except to look after the house and me. I shouldn't have thought I was much bother!'

'If it wasn't for you, my boy, I could go out and get a good job,' said his mother. 'And one of these days I will, if you don't do what you're told. I'd like to earn good money and have something to spend on better clothes and go to a dance at times, and to the cinema more often. But I can't because I've got you to see to. And all you do is to defy me and be rude.'

Bob was shocked. *Was* he such a nuisance and a bother? He couldn't be! He saw that his mother was upset and he went to her. He put his arm round her waist and gave her a hug.

'Don't take on so, Mum,' he said. 'I'm a good boy at heart! Go on, smile at me! You're all I've got, Mum, you know you are – and I wouldn't hurt you for worlds!'

'Well, you come home when you're told, then,' said his mother. 'And don't press me so hard with your arm.'

Bob let go and stood back, hurt. He really loved his mother, and always wished she would be more loving to him. He knew she was proud of him and his good looks and self-confidence, but he wanted more than that. He wanted her love too – and, like Tom, he compared her with Mrs Mackenzie.

The twins' mother was always so kind, Bob thought. She always seemed so pleased to see them whenever they came back from school. She didn't mind hugging them back when they hugged her. He was quite sure they never seemed a bother to her. She was a *real* mother.

He felt his heart sink suddenly. Wasn't his mother a real mother? Was he a nuisance now that she hadn't got his father? He knew that money had been tight since his father died – but he had left them enough to be comfortably off. He felt impelled to hug his mother again, hoping that this time she would hug him back, and prove his thoughts wrong.

She gave him a small hug but that was all. Then she smiled at him brightly. 'Well now, Bob – you seem as if you're sorry for going against my wishes and coming home so late. Don't do it again, will you?'

Bob took away his arm. He looked surly now. 'I

shan't promise,' he said, and turned away. 'I'm not a baby. And I won't be a nuisance either! You get me sandwiches for my lunch each day and I won't need to come home to dinner.'

He didn't for one moment think that his mother would take him at his word. He enjoyed coming home in the middle of the day and telling all that had happened, even if his mother didn't seem to listen very much. He liked calling for the Mackenzies in the afternoon and stroking Frisky and taking little Pat by the hand.

So he was horrified the next morning when he suddenly saw his mother cutting up sandwiches in the kitchen. He stared at them and then at her.

'Who are they for, Mum?' he asked, afraid.

'For you,' said his mother, cutting the bread squares in half. 'How many do you want?'

'But Mum – I didn't mean it!' cried Bob. 'I didn't think you'd do it!'

'Well now you see I have,' said his mother. 'If you so badly want to spend all your time at school you can.'

'But *I* don't want to,' said Bob desperately. 'I only said that because you said I was a nuisance.'

'It's quite a good idea, really,' said Mrs Kent, not looking at Bob. 'It means I can sometimes go off for the day and see my friends in Croydon. I feel so cut off down here. Look, do you think that's enough?'

'Mum, you go off for the day when you want to,' said Bob, pulling at his mother's arm. 'But let me come home the other days. I tell you I only *said* that.'

'You're getting to be a difficult boy,' said Mrs Kent, cutting a piece of cake and wrapping it up with the sandwiches. 'If your father had been alive he would have whipped you many a time for your disobedience. You're so bossy too – thinking you can have everything your own way! And anyway I don't know why you're making such a fuss, Bob; lots of other children stay to dinner at school.'

'Yes. But I don't *need* to,' said Bob, making a last desperate effort. 'Do I, Mum? I *like* coming home. I *want* to come home, like the Mackenzies do.'

'I can't imagine why Mrs Mackenzie doesn't let all her three take sandwiches,' said Mrs Kent, tying string round the packet. 'On top of her all the time! One's trouble enough – but three! There you are, there's plenty there for you. I'll see you at tea-time.'

There was nothing more to be said. If Bob was determined and obstinate, so was his mother! Bob went off, upset. He tried to comfort himself by thinking that his mother was just punishing him for being late the night before – but he had a most uncomfortable feeling that it was more than a punishment. She was glad to be rid of him for the day!

He walked alone to school that morning, thinking hard. Was he annoying to his mother? Didn't she like him to look after her as he tried to do? Was he really 'too big for his boots'? His heart sunk again when he remembered her hard voice. He must do his best to show her that he loved her and wanted his home. It was quite unthinkable that his mother wanted to be rid of him. That would mean she didn't love him.

He didn't hear the Mackenzies calling him. He walked on, his head down, puzzled and worried. Then he heard quick footsteps and a small hand was thrust into his. It was Pat!

He looked down, smiling, his heart lifting at once. He squeezed Pat's hand tightly and hurt her. But she didn't mind, because it told her that Bob liked her so much. She began to chatter to him, and he found his worries going.

He got them all back again, though, at lunch-time.

He set off to the cloakroom to get his cap and coat with Jeanie and Donald — and suddenly remembered that he wasn't going home! He was to stay at school with the dinner-boys and girls and eat his sandwiches.

'I forgot — I'm staying at school for dinner today,' he said to Donald, and went back to the classroom.

'See you this afternoon then,' called Donald, and off he went with Jeanie and Pat. Tom, Eleanor and Hilda went with them. Bob watched them from the window, enviously.

'I'll buy Mum some flowers,' he thought suddenly. 'I've got 10p. Surely that would buy a few flowers for her? She'll like that.'

So after school that afternoon he went to the little flower shop and looked at the flowers. How dreadfully expensive they were! Good gracious — he could never afford those prices!

The shop-girl saw him looking dismally in at the door and she called to him. 'What do you want? A bunch of flowers?'

'Well, I wanted to buy some for my mother, but they're all so expensive,' said Bob.

'How much do you want to spend?' said the girl.

'I've only got 10p,' said Bob.

'I'll make you up a nice little bunch of violets for 10p,' said the girl. She got up and took some violets from a bowl of water. She set the stalks together and twisted a bit of cotton round them, and then surrounded the little purple bunch with big green leaves.

'Smell,' she said. 'They're lovely. My, your mother is lucky to have a nice boy like you taking her flowers! She'll give you a big hug, I'm sure.'

Bob smiled politely. He hoped she was right. He gave the girl his 10p and set off. He ran most of the way home, feeling as if he had been away for a week!

He rushed in at the back door, calling loudly, 'Mum! Where are you, Mum?'

He heard voices in the sitting-room. He slammed the back door and rushed in. 'Mum! Look what I've got for you!'

An old friend of his mother's was sitting there, drinking tea. She put her cup down hurriedly as Bob rushed in. He took no notice of her at all.

'Look,' he said, and held out the little bunch of violets to his mother. She took them and set them on her tea-tray.

'Bob, what a way to come in!' she said. 'Can't you see I have a visitor here – dear Mrs Adams, all the way from Croydon to see us! Where are your manners?'

Bob could have burst with rage. To think that this old lady, who he had always thoroughly disliked, should be there to tea with his mother, when he so badly wanted to fuss her and give her flowers and make her be nice to him! And all his mother had done was to take his flowers and put them aside without even saying thank you. Bob went crimson with disappointment.

'Shake hands with Mrs Adams, Bob,' said his mother, sounding cross. How annoying of Bob to come rushing in like that, his hands dirty, his hair untidy!

He shook hands with the disapproving old lady, and mumbled something.

'I don't think it's improving him, coming down here,' said Mrs Adams looking at Bob critically. 'And from what you tell me of his behaviour I'm afraid the new friends he has made aren't doing him any good.'

Bob stared at her, shocked and angry. 'What has my mother been telling you about me?' he demanded.

'Now, now Bob – sit down and have some tea,' said his mother, annoyed with Mrs Adams for telling Bob that she had been complaining of him, and annoyed with Bob for looking so untidy and forgetting his manners.

'I don't want any tea,' said Bob, rudely. He just stopped himself from putting out his tongue at the shocked Mrs Adams, and then he rushed out of the room at top speed. SLAM went the door behind him!

## CHAPTER SIX

## Bob Lets Off Steam

Mrs Adams was really shocked. 'What a naughty boy!' she said. 'So different from when I knew him last year. Dear dear – it just shows how badly a boy needs a father, doesn't it? Such a good looking little fellow, too.'

Mrs Kent was very angry with Bob. How dared he behave like that? She debated with herself whether to go and fetch him and make him apologize? Then she decided not to. Bob had such a temper. He really was making things difficult lately.

She opened her heart to old Mrs Adams. How tied she was now with a big boy like Bob to see to – and such a difficult boy too! She could never see her old friends, never take a nice holiday, never buy herself the pretty things she wanted to buy.

'If only I could get a job, I could earn good money,' said Mrs Kent, dabbing her eyes. 'Lots of mothers do. Then I could at least have a change from the house, and give myself – and Bob too, of course – little treats.'

'Well, why don't you?' said Mrs Adams, taking a little cake. 'What's to stop you? You're your own mistress, aren't you? That boy of yours doesn't deserve to have you giving up all your freedom for him. He's a bad boy, *I* think. You'll have to keep a firm hand on him.'

Mrs Kent was torn between her pride in her boy's good looks and upright bearing, and her annoyance at his behaviour. She caught sight of the violets on the tea-tray and suddenly felt sorry. She picked them up and smelt them.

'Don't you get taken in by little things like those violets,' said Mrs Adams, who had taken a great dislike to Bob. 'He's probably done something wrong, and that's his way of putting you off. *I* know boys! I've had four of my own, and I know their little ways.'

Mrs Kent put the violets down again. She heard the front door slam and saw Bob running down the path. He disappeared for a moment and then she saw him going into the Mackenzies' garden. She felt cross.

'Now he'll have tea there and be made a fuss of and not come home for ages,' she thought. And probably this is just exactly what *would* have happened, if all the Mackenzies hadn't happened to be out on a visit to their Granny.

There was no one at home, not even Frisky. Bob turned away from the back door, disconsolate. Everything was against him! Not even little Pat was there to slip her hand in his.

He climbed over the fence and went to the shed in his own garden. He slipped inside and sat down. He had had no tea, but he didn't feel hungry. He began to brood.

He waited till he heard old Mrs Adams going, and then he slipped into the kitchen. He waited till his mother came out. She looked at him, and he flung himself on her.

'Mum, I'm sorry! I hate that nasty old woman! You

shouldn't have told her bad things about me. I wanted so badly to see you and give you those violets.'

'I would prefer good behaviour to violets, Bob,' said his mother, but she sounded kinder. He hugged her till she could hardly breathe.

'Mum, I'm not really bad, I'll do all I can,' said Bob. 'Did you miss me at dinner-time? I missed you!'

'Now don't let's talk any more about it,' said his mother. 'Do you want any tea? There is still some left on the table. Go and wash, Bob – you look awful. And your hair!'

Bob went to wash. He felt happier, but he wanted something he hadn't been able to get. He wanted a warm response from his mother. She *was* kinder – but she wasn't warm, like Mrs Mackenzie was when anyone hugged her. Blow! He mustn't keep comparing his mother to Mrs Mackenzie. He'd try like anything now to make his mother love him and be proud of him.

He did his best that evening. His mother had to laugh at the things he did. He brought enough wood and coal in to last for a week. He did all the washing-up. He cleaned her dirty shoes and her clean ones too. He put two hot-water bottles in her bed instead of one. If ever a boy showed kindness to his mother, Bob was that boy.

Mrs Kent put the violets in water, and said thank you Bob, but no more. He went to bed early so that she wouldn't have to nag him to go. He lay and hoped that she would come and kiss him good-night. But she didn't come. She hardly ever had come, but tonight Bob thought somehow she might.

'Perhaps she thinks I'm too big now,' he thought sorrowfully. 'And I *am* big, of course. But I know Mrs Mackenzie always kisses the twins good-night. She never misses. They told me so. I do *think* Mum could have come just this once, when I've shown her I'm sorry.'

Bob didn't tell anyone of the upset he had had with his mother. He was very subdued when he went to school the next morning.

Pat wondered what was the matter.

The matter was that his mother had packed his lunch for him again! Bob had thought she wouldn't – she would let him come home to dinner as usual. She would forgive him and let things be the same.

But she hadn't. She had packed up his sandwiches and given them to him – and Bob hadn't said a word. All right, if she didn't want him home, he wouldn't come!

Pat went to Jeanie and Donald. 'What's the matter with Bob?' she said. 'He didn't even *notice* me this morning. He looks so peculiar, and he won't smile at all.'

Jeanie and Donald had also noticed something wrong. Jeanie went up to Bob. 'Hallo, Bob!' she said, cheerfully. 'You look like a hen left out in the rain! What's gone wrong? Forgotten your homework?'

Bob shook himself. He made himself smile, and then he felt as if he suddenly didn't care about anything at all, not even his mother! He gave a loud whoop and began to act the clown. He could do this very well indeed, and he made the others laugh. Soon he had a little group round him, egging him on.

'Go it, Bob!' said Tom. 'Fall over yourself again! How do you do it?'

Something mad entered into Bob that morning. He irritated the teachers intensely. He was cheeky and disobedient. He arranged a pile of books on his desk, and every time he stood up to answer a question, he joggled his desk so that the books toppled over.

CRASH! The books lay scattered on the floor. The children, who had watched Bob build up the pile of books while the teacher was writing on the board, giggled in delight.

'What is the matter with you this morning, Bob Kent?' said the teacher at last. 'Do you want me to send you to the Head?'

Bob really felt at that moment as if he didn't care where he was sent — but he felt a nudge from someone beside him, Harry, a boy he liked. Harry had enjoyed his antics immensely but he could see trouble ahead for anyone who was getting as far beyond himself as Bob. He would end in being sent to the Head, and that would mean serious trouble.

'Don't be a fathead,' whispered Harry.

So Bob didn't say, 'Yes, Miss Roland, I'd love to be sent to the Head,' as his tongue wanted him to say. He simply said, 'No, thank you, Miss Roland.'

'Then sit down and behave yourself,' said Miss Roland sharply. Bob sat down — but he didn't exactly behave himself. He carefully inked a piece of paper on one side, then turned it upside down, held it by a dry corner and handed it to the boy in front of him.

But before George could take it, Miss Roland's sharp eyes saw the paper.

'Bob!' she rapped out. 'What are you passing notes for?'

'Please, Miss Roland, I'm not,' said Bob.

'Why, I *saw* you,' said Miss Roland, crossly. 'Bring the note here.'

All the children held their breath as Bob walked up to the desk. They knew perfectly well that the paper was covered with wet ink underneath. Miss Roland held out her hand for it.

She took it — and immediately felt the wet ink on the under-side. She turned it over in disgust. Her fingers were covered with blue ink!

Two or three children gave helpless giggles. Miss Roland looked coldly at Bob. 'I suppose you think this kind of thing is funny?' she said.

'I do, rather,' said Bob, honestly. There were more giggles. Miss Roland glared round.

'One more sound from any of you and I shall keep everyone in for twenty minutes after school!' she said. There was dead silence at once.

'I think you'd better go out of the room, Bob,' she said. 'The Head will be coming along the corridor soon, and he will no doubt ask you a few questions when he sees you standing outside the door. I'm ashamed of your behaviour this morning. I really can't think what's the matter with you.'

Bob walked out of the room, bestowing winks all the way. Nobody dared to wink back. Miss Roland was now on the war-path, and it would be dangerous to make her any angrier that she already was.

As soon as Bob got outside the room, all his mad excitement went. He leaned moodily against the wall. His worries came back, and he kicked savagely at the wall as he suddenly remembered old Mrs Adams. His mother shouldn't have said horrid things about him to that nasty old woman. It was disloyal of her!

He heard footsteps and wondered if it was the Head coming along. In his present gloomy mood he didn't want any more trouble. He glanced round and saw a cupboard where brooms and brushes were kept. He went to it and opened the door. Good! There was just enough room to squeeze in and hide.

So when the Head came striding down the corridor there was no Bob to be seen! He was inside the cupboard, holding his breath, not feeling nearly so bold and brave as he had done a few minutes before in the classroom. He needed the admiration and laughter and encouragement of the others to keep his boldness going! He crouched there, his heart beating uncomfortably fast.

The footsteps paused, and Bob didn't dare to move even an eyelash. The Head was listening to the chanting of some poem in the classroom.

Then the footsteps went out again and Bob breathed freely. He stayed in the cupboard, however, till the end of the class. Then, when the bell went for Break and the others poured out, he slipped out and joined them. They surounded him thumping him on the back.

'How you made us laugh, Bob! *Did* you see Miss Roland's face when she got ink all over her hand? Oh Bob, how *dared* you?'

<br>

CHAPTER SEVEN

## 'You Go Behind my Back!'

Bob was quite the hero of the day. The story of his idiotic behaviour in class flew through the school. Tom came up and grinned at him.

'I wish you were in *my* class, Bob,' he said. 'You might liven things up a bit. Our master's deadly dull!'

Bob's spirits had perked up again with all the admiration and laughter, but not quite to such a pitch as before. He worked off some of his strange mood in Break, dashing about all over the place, shouting, jumping, and chasing the smaller ones till they yelled, half-thrilled, half-fearful.

'Coming home with us today, Bob?' asked Donald, as they went in to school again. 'You stayed here yesterday dinner-time, didn't you?'

For some reason Bob didn't want to say that his

mother had packed him up sandwiches again, and that he had to stay at school. He found himself saying something unexpected.

'No, I'm not staying at school for dinner. I got my mother to put me up some lunch, and I'm going to take it down to the canal to eat. I like watching the barges there.'

'You're lucky!' said Donald enviously, and that made Bob feel better, though why he didn't know.

That was the beginning of Bob's strange, lonely lunches. Each day he went off with the others, left them at the road that led down to the canal, and went off to find his favourite corner there. He ate his sandwiches all by himself, staring at the barges that went smoothly by.

He didn't tell his mother what he was doing. Why should he, he thought. He felt vaguely that he was somehow 'getting back at her' by not eating his sandwiches at school, but crouching down by the canal.

One morning it rained heavily. He had to find a place to shelter in, and discovered a little shed full of odds and ends of things, belonging to one of the warehouses. It was locked, but he could climb in through the window.

He ate his lunch in the half-darkness there, and afterwards, bored, he began to look through the things in the shed. There were pots of paint and brushes, and bottles of various kinds, rope, tins full and empty, a barrel or two, and wooden boxes.

A shout made him jump. An angry face was peering through the window.

'What are you doing in there? Come on out of it! Don't you know what you'll get if you steal things?'

'I'm *not* stealing,' said Bob, indignantly. 'I only came in here because of the rain.'

'Oh yes! I've heard that tale before,' said the man. 'I suppose you climbed in through the window. Now you look here, young fellow, I'll let you off this time — but if I see you in this shed again, or hanging about to see what you can lay your hands on, I'll report you to the police.'

He unlocked the door of the shed, and as Bob ran out he gave him a cuff. The boy was furious and resentful. He hadn't done any harm in the shed!

That day, quite innocently, Jeanie gave his secret away. She had really believed that Bob had asked his mother to give him sandwiches to eat by the canal. On this rainy day she remembered Bob, and wondered if he had as usual slipped down to the canal.

'I hope Bob's found somewhere to shelter,' she said,

looking at the rain pelting down. 'He'll get wet down by the canal.'

'Whatever is he doing by the canal today?' said Mrs Mackenzie in astonishment. 'Isn't he home for his dinner as usual?'

'Oh no, Mother. His mother packs him up sandwiches, because he likes to go and have them by the canal,' said Jeanie, cutting up her meat.

'He likes to watch the barges,' added Pat. 'He told me so.'

'Well, I think he ought to go home in *this* weather!' said Mrs Mackenzie. 'His mother will be very worried about him.'

And when she happened to meet Mrs Kent that afternoon, Mrs Mackenzie spoke about Bob and his dinner! 'I hope Bob had the sense to come home to his dinner today,' she said. 'How odd these boys are, aren't they, wanting to go down to the canal whenever they can!'

Mrs Kent looked astonished. 'To the *canal*?' she said. 'Bob doesn't go there. He takes sandwiches to school and has them there with the others. It was his own idea!'

Mrs Mackenzie said no more, but she was puzzled. Mrs Kent, however, said a lot when Bob came home that afternoon when school was over.

'What's this I hear about you taking your lunch down to the canal?' she demanded, as soon as Bob came in. Bob looked up sharply.

'Who told you that?' he asked.

'Never you mind,' said his mother. '*Do* you go? You know you're supposed to have it at school. I won't have you wandering about in the dinner-hour like that. Whatever will people say? They'll want to know why you aren't at home!'

'If you give me sandwiches I shall have my dinner where I like,' said Bob, obstinately.

But he was wrong there! His mother promptly went to the school, saw the Headmaster, and asked him to see that Bob was kept at school during the lunch-hour with the other dinner-children.

'He asked me to let him take sandwiches,' said Mrs Kent, not altogether untruthfully, 'and I suppose he thinks he can wander off on his own. He's a difficult boy, Mr Williams – likes his own way too much. He wants a firm hand.'

'Yes. I've not had very good reports of Bob lately, I'm afraid,' said the Head. 'Nothing very *bad*, you understand; mostly mischief and showing off to the others. Playing the idiot. All right, Mrs Kent, I'll see that he stays here at lunch-time. But he used to go home to his dinner, didn't he? Wouldn't you rather he came home each day again, so that you yourself could keep an eye on him?'

'Well, no,' said Mrs Kent. 'You see – I'm thinking of taking up some work, Mr Williams, and I might not be at home,'

'I see,' said Mr Williams. 'Very well – we'll keep an eye on Bob for you.'

So Bob found that he was stopped when he was slipping off with the others the next day. 'You're to stay here, Bob,' said Mr Kennet, the master on duty.

'Who said so?' asked Bob, in a flash.

'Your mother, I believe?' said Mr Kennet. 'Take your sandwiches over with the other children – and don't glare like that!'

Bob could hardly wait till he got home that afternoon! He was so angry. His mother had been behind his back, and goodness knew what she had said, and she hadn't even told him about it! He burst into the house and slammed the door behind him.

'Don't, Bob!' said his mother, startled.

'Why didn't you tell me you'd been to the school and stopped me from taking my lunch out?' burst out Bob. 'You're mean. You go behind my back! I wasn't doing any harm, taking my sandwiches down to the canal!'

'Now then, Bob, don't you talk to me like that,' said Mrs Kent. 'How dare you! If your father was alive he'd give you a good hiding!'

'I wouldn't mind how many hidings he gave me, if only he was alive!' shouted Bob. 'He wouldn't treat me like you do – pushing me off for dinner, and then going behind my back! I won't . . .'

'Stop shouting at me like that,' said his mother, shocked and angry. 'I didn't hear very good things about you from the Head! He's not at all pleased with you, he said. You've been . . .'

'So you've both been saying things against me,' said Bob, bitterly. 'You ought to back me up, Mum. Let me come back home to dinner again, and I won't go off on my own. Go on – you let me. I'll feel different then.'

'All you want is to get your own way,' said his mother, a hard note in her voice. 'You can't come home to dinner, for a very good reason. I probably shan't be here to dinnner myself soon.'

Bob stared at her, astonished. 'Why? What's happening?'

'I think I shall soon find a job to do,' said his mother. 'I'm bored now. And I want a bit more money.'

'Don't do that,' said Bob, suddenly filled with panic, though he didn't know why. 'I like to think of you at home all day. I don't want to think of an empty house – and no fire – and no kettle boiling. Don't you get a job, Mum. I'll do anything you want me to. I won't even ask to come home to dinner, if you won't get a job. Can't you wait a few years till I'm old enough to earn money for you? I'll . . .'

'Oh, don't go on so, Bob,' said his mother. 'You make my head ache. Fancy talking of earning money, when you're only a child – and a silly one at that. You think yourself so big and such a man, and want to have everything your own way. Well, you've got to learn you can't.'

'You're not to go out to work, Mum,' cried Bob. 'You've got enough money – I've heard you say you have. You're not to go!'

'That's enough,' said his mother, getting up and pushing him away. 'Telling me what I'm to do and not to do! I never heard anything like it. You're too big for your boots altogether.'

Bob watched his mother go out of the room. He felt suddenly insecure. He looked round the cosy room – the fire burning brightly, the table laid for tea, flowers here and there. He had a sudden vision of it cold and empty, with no bustling sounds coming from the kitchen. He didn't like it at all.

He ate his tea without tasting it. He looked anxiously at his silent mother, sipping her tea and looking into the fire.

'Can I do something for you, Mum?' he asked at last, feeling that if he could just do something, preferably something difficult, it might make things better.

His mother shook her head. 'No,' she said. 'I don't want anything done.'

But Bob couldn't sit and do nothing that night. He went out to the shed and he took down the chopper. He chopped wood until his arm was tired. Chop, chop, chop!

'What *is* Bob doing, chopping away like that?' said Mrs Mackenzie, next door. 'What a good boy he is to be sure!'

## CHAPTER EIGHT

# *The Big Row*

And how was the family at Summerhayes getting on? Certainly no better! They were well settled in now, and although the children were quite used to the smaller rooms and garden, Mrs Berkeley wasn't!

Her husband began to feel that for the rest of his life he would hear moans and groans about the lovely house they used to have! Even Eleanor and Hilda got tired of it.

'Mother, don't keep on so,' said Eleanor, one day when her mother had been grumbling because she was ashamed of asking her old friends to see her in her new small house. 'If our old friends really *are* our friends they'll love to come here. What does it matter what they think, anyway?'

'It's not what *they* think that matters, it's what *I* think!' said Mrs Berkeley. 'And don't you go turning against me, Eleanor.'

'I'm not, Mother,' said Eleanor. 'But really, you do go on and on about things!'

'Don't be rude, Eleanor,' said her mother. 'I shall tell your father about you.'

'All right,' said Eleanor, tired of the continual nagging. 'He thinks the same as I do — you go on and on about things. I don't wonder sometimes that he walks out of the room.'

'Nor do I,' said Hilda, unexpectedly. 'We never, never have any — any *peace* in this house, Mother. Why

53

can't we be like the Mackenzies? Jeanie's mother doesn't go on about things.'

'You're both unkind, rude girls,' said her mother, angry. 'As for those Mackenzies, don't let me hear about them again! Paragons! Always doing the right thing and never complaining and never gossiping – just like cabbages, sitting there contented, no matter what happens!'

'Oh Mother! Mrs Mackenzie isn't a cabbage!' said Hilda, with a laugh that made Mrs Berkeley angry. 'Why, she's always on the go. She's running the Sale of Work, and she's helping to make the dresses for our school play, and Mr Mackenzie is making some of the properties. He wants Dad to help him.'

'Oh yes, they're full of Good Works,' said Mrs Berkeley in a shaking voice that told the girls she was about to burst into tears. 'I hate people who are full of Good Works, especially when they are pushed down my throat!'

'But *Mother*!' said Eleanor, puzzled. '*Somebody* has got to do these things, surely – and it means a lot of work and giving up time. Anyway, I *like* the Mackenzies. They all pull together.'

'I shall tell your father about you tonight,' said her mother. 'I don't know what things are coming to – Tom always so surly, and now you two getting rude. I did think *you* were on my side.'

'All this business of taking sides!' said Eleanor. 'Why have we got to? I think sometimes this is an awful home. I'll jolly well leave as soon as I'm old enough and go somewhere where there's a bit of peace.'

She stalked out of the room just as her father came in. He went hurriedly out again as soon as he sensed the atmosphere of the sitting-room.

'Dad! Mother's going to complain about me and Hilda

to you tonight,' said Eleanor. 'And Tom too, I expect. Can't you make her settle down and be happy? It makes things awful for everyone.'

The row that night was never forgotten. The three children were already in bed when it happened, but they could hear the raised voices downstairs and they were frightened. Suppose Mother threw something at Dad? She did get so angry sometimes.

The two girls got out of bed and huddled together on the top stairs, listening. They were too worried to think of putting on their dressing-gowns, and they shivered.

Tom soon joined them. He was shivering too, partly with cold, partly with fear. These dreadful rows! They all put their arms round one another for warmth, and for once in a way the three were united. A thought passed through Hilda's mind. Hadn't the three of them better stick together, instead of quarrelling as they so often did? This was such a dreadful house for taking sides!

The voices were raised again. Their father was shouting. 'If things don't get different, if you don't stop this nagging and bickering, I shall clear out. You're always putting the children against me – even my own son that I want to be proud of! I can't stand it much longer. Do you want a broken home? You're breaking it up with your behaviour!'

The children sat tense. Dad mustn't go away! They were often rude and unkind to him and sided with their mother, but they couldn't think of home without Dad coming back at night, giving them their pocket money on Saturday, reading their school reports to them, dressing the Christmas tree at Christmas, and bathing with them at the seaside in the summer. He was part of the Family.

'What do you mean?' came their mother's voice. 'A broken home! Now you just tell me what you mean by that!'

'I'll tell you,' said their father, his voice coming clearly up the stairs to the listening children. 'It's a home like ours where the parents don't pull together, where they quarrel in front of the children, and where everyone takes sides against somebody else. It says in the Bible that a house divided against itself cannot stand. It must fall. A broken household, a broken home, makes children go wrong, it ruins them, it . . .'

'Stop!' cried Mrs Berkeley, 'how dare you say that our children will go wrong!'

'Well, you've been telling tales about them to me all the evening,' said Mr Berkeley. 'Talking about their misdeeds! Poor kids, they never get a chance of settling down in peace and serenity. They're not happy. One of these days they *will* go wrong, as so many children do in an unhappy home.'

The three children shivered together. This was dreadful. Who was right, their mother or their father? They were muddled. They didn't know. And then they heard a sound that struck despair into their hearts.

Slam! That was the front door banging. They heard their father's footsteps going down the front path into the night. Hilda and Eleanor began to cry. Tom gave them a rough hug. He wanted to cry too, but he was a boy, so he stared fiercely down the stairs and wondered desperately what to do.

Eleanor got up. She went up to the landing and into her room. Hilda followed her. Tom hesitated. Should he go down to his mother? No, he couldn't. The thought of prolonged tears and complaints sickened him. Suppose his father didn't come back? Suppose he really had done what he threatened to do, and had 'cleared out'?

Tom peeped into his sisters' room. The light of a street-lamp came through the window, and the boy saw the two girls kneeling beisde their bed. He heard what Hilda was saying over and over again.

'Please God, let Dad come back. Please God, let Dad come back.'

For a moment Tom felt savage. Why couldn't his parents agree? Why did people marry if they weren't going to help one another and make their children happy? Tom couldn't understand it. He went into his room, shut the door and got into bed. He had no pity and no love for his parents at all at that moment. He disliked them both.

Tom fell asleep, but the girls kept awake, listening for footsteps coming up the garden path. And at last they heard them! Thank goodness Dad had come back. They heard the key in the lock. They heard the door open.

But their father didn't go into the sitting-room where their mother still sat. He went straight upstairs to his room, went in and shut the door. Soon afterwards they heard the creak of his bed. Would their mother come up now? They lay and whispered, waiting for more sounds. They fell asleep without hearing anything further, and slept soundly till the morning, tired out with anxiety.

In the morning three subdued children crept down to breakfast, white-faced, and fearful. Their father had already left to catch the early train. Only their mother was there, cooking the breakfast, looking pale and red-eyed.

Nobody said anything. The children gobbled their breakfasts as quickly as possible, and collected their school things. Anything to get out of the house quickly! They heaved sighs of relief when at last they were on

the road to school. No more storms had burst at breakfast. Their mother hadn't said a word. She had looked
hurt and grieved that not one of the children had said
anything, but they were all too afraid of another upset.

'Thank goodness for school!' said Hilda. 'Dear old
school!'

'Yes, I even feel glad of French and Maths,' said
Eleanor.

'And I'm glad it's games this afternoon,' said Tom.
'I wish I was like Bob, and could have my dinner
at school! I don't believe he likes being made to have
his sandwiches there, but I wouldn't mind!'

Their teacher saw that Hilda and Eleanor were pale
and worried. She spoke to one of the other teachers
about it.

'Those poor kids have been through another upset
at home, I suppose,' she said. 'I know someone who
used to live near them in Croydon and she told me
that there was never a moment's peace there! We can't
expect either Hilda or Eleanor to do much in class today!'

They didn't, of course. They were tired, and worried
at having to go home to dinner while the atmosphere
of home was all upset. But to the girls' pleasant surprise
no one scolded them for inattention, and nobody even
seemed to notice when Hilda got all her sums wrong.

As for Tom, he was like Bob. When things went
wrong he went wrong too, and was silly and rude and
showed off. It was his way of trying to forget, his
way of saying to the world, 'What! You're trying to
get me down, are you? Well, I'll show you! I'll get
*you* down instead! I'll fight you, see?'

So he was extremely trying that morning, and if the
word hadn't gone round that the Berkeleys must have
had another of their family rows, he would most
certainly have been severely punished.

But he wasn't. 'I'd like to punish his parents instead though!' said his master. 'I'd keep them in for a month!'

## CHAPTER NINE

## An Evening Out

That night Tom didn't want to be at home for the evening. He knew that his mother and father probably wouldn't be on speaking terms, and he decided to keep away.

'I'm going round to Bob's to see his clockwork railway going,' he said to his mother gruffly, and went out before she could say a word. He wasn't really going to Bob's. He meant to wander about till it was time to go to bed.

And quite unexpectedly he bumped into Bob! Bob had had the same idea. His mother had just told him that she had applied for a job, and if she was accepted she would take it. Bob had rushed out of the house, unable to say another word.

The boys met round a corner. 'Sorry,' said Bob as he collided with Tom. Tom recognized his voice. He was pleased. He admired Bob and his boldness and cheek.

'Hallo, Bob!' he said. 'What are *you* doing here?'

'Just out by myself,' said Bob. 'Where are you going?'

'Nowhere in particular,' said Tom. 'We've had a row at home, so I cleared out. I'm fed up. You had a row too!'

'Not exactly,' said Bob, not liking to say anything against his mother, but glad of a little sympathy and company. 'Things do go wrong sometimes, don't they?'

'Well, *I* can't do anything right at the moment,' said Tom, 'and I'm not staying at home to be rowed all the time. You haven't got a father, have you? Well, you're lucky, because then your mother can't have rows with him!'

'My mother and father never did have rows,' said Bob, 'and I'd give anything to have him back again. Things are much better with a father around.'

'Depends on the father,' said Tom, feeling rather big to be able to talk about parents in this way. 'I say – it's beginning to rain.'

'What shall we do?' said Bob. 'We can't mess about in the rain. I was rather thinking of going down to the canal and getting on board a barge that's lying there. Nobody's on it. We could have explored a bit.'

'Well, we can't now that it's pouring with rain,' said Tom. 'But I don't particularly want to go back home, do you?'

'No,' said Bob, decidedly.

'Got any money?' said Tom. 'We could go to the cinema. There's a good picture on.'

'I've only a coin or two,' said Bob. 'It *would* be nice to go to the cinema. It's warm in there, and you can forget everything except the picture.'

'Yes. A chap has got to forget things when they get bad,' said Tom, putting his arm through Bob's. 'I've got no money, either. It's in my money-box at home, but I don't want to go back and get it. Still – we could get in without money!'

'How?' asked Bob, puzzled.

'There's a little door at the back,' said Tom, lowering his voice. 'I found it by accident one day. It wasn't locked. If we choose a moment to go in when there's a lot of banging and shooting going on, nobody would hear us. It leads into a small passage, and if nobody's about we can slip into the main passage and down into side-seats without being seen. I've done it before.'

'But – ought we to?' asked Bob.

'Go on! Don't say you're afraid!' said Tom, scornfully. 'I thought you were full of pluck – didn't mind anything!'

'Well, I don't,' said Bob, immediately thinking of this exploit as something daring, and not as something wrong. 'Come on – I'm game. But let's be careful.'

They ran through the pouring rain and came to the big brightly-lit cinema. They slipped round the side into a big yard. Tom led the way to a small door right at the back. He tried the handle cautiously.

'It's not locked,' he whispered. 'Now – as soon as

we hear music or noises from the picture, we'll slip in. Hang on to me.'

Tom turned the handle, the door opened silently. The boys slipped inside and shut the door. They were in a little passage. Tom tiptoed down it in the darkness towards a doorway that was dimly outlined. He cautiously peeped round it into another passage.

Nobody was there. The boys slid along it in the shadows and came to a small side door that led into the cinema at one side. Tom waited till he could hear loud noises on the screen, and then he opened the door.

The side-seats were very near. No attendant was to be seen. They were all taking tickets at the top end of the cinema, or showing people to their seats in the darkness.

Tom and Bob crouched low and went to the nearby seats. They chose two by the wall, where it was very dark because of a wide pillar. They sank into them thankfully, their hearts beating fast. Tom let out a long breath.

'Well, here we are!' he whispered. 'Not a bad idea, is it?'

Bob didn't answer. He was already lost in the picture. It was one that children were not allowed to see unless they had a grown-up with them. The boys had not looked at the posters outside and had not seen that the picture was one for adults, certainly not for children too.

It was an exciting picture, the boys thought. There was plenty of shooting and chasing and hiding. There was also a lot of kissing, which bored the two boys very much. They glued their eyes to the picture, clenching their fists at the shooting parts, and hardly breathing when a great chase was going on.

'I wish we'd seen the beginning,' whispered Tom,

when the picture came to an end. 'Shall we sit round the programme and see the start of this picture, so that we know what happened? We can see it all through again if you like.'

'No, my mother would be worried,' whispered back Bob. 'But we can see just the beginning of it, if you like. Shut up now – the cartoon is beginning.'

They roared at the antics shown in the cartoon, and felt very much better for their laughter. Things didn't seem so worrying when you had had a good laugh. Both boys stopped thinking about the scolding they would get when they went home.

The programme was a continuous one, but the lights came up between the short picture and the long one. They went up suddenly when a picture had ended, and the boys all at once found the cinema flooded with light. They hadn't even time to duck, because they had not been expecting this.

'Sit absolutely still,' hissed Tom, scared. 'No one will notice us then. Don't bob about or try to hide.'

No attendant noticed them. But someone in the audience did! A woman was there, idly looking over the crowd with her friend. She suddenly saw the two boys over in the corner. She nudged her companion.

'Just look over there! This is a picture for *Adults only* – and the management has let in those two boys. Neither of them can be anything like sixteen! It's a scandal, breaking the law like that! I shall complain!'

And she got up, made her way out of the row of seats and went to find the manager. He saw her in his office, wondering what her complaint was.

'This is a picture for adults,' began the woman. 'And quite right too. It's not fit for children to see. But you've let in two boys together, and neither of them can be anything like sixteen years old — which is the age they must be to see this picture by themselves!'

'Madam, we are very strict about that law,' said the manager. 'I can assure you that no child is let into my theatre to see an *adult* picture unless he is accompanied by a *grown-up* who is responsible for him. Not that that makes the picture any more suitable for him, I quite agree.'

'The point is that you *have* let in two youngsters!' said the woman. 'Come and look.'

She took the manager to the top of the cinema. The lights were still on, but went off as they got there. The woman pointed to where Tom and Bob were sitting.

'You can just see them, even now,' she said. 'There — now the picture is very bright — can you see them? Two quite small boys — one doesn't look more than ten!'

The manager saw them and frowned. 'Thank you, madam,' he said. 'You are right, they are small boys; but you are wrong to say we let them in. We didn't. They must have crept in somewhere from the back of the theatre without paying. I'll call the police.'

'No, don't. Please don't do that!' said the woman, in alarm. 'I don't want to hand the boys over to the police. Can't you deal with them yourself? Give them a fright, so that they won't do such a thing again?'

The manager hesitated. Then he nodded. 'All right — I'll deal with them myself. I've got kids of my own, and I can't say that I'd like any of them to be handed over to the police. I'll catch these little monkeys myself and find out who they are.'

And so, when the picture was just getting to the part where Bob and Tom had come in, they suddenly heard a stern voice near by.

'What are you doing here?'

The boys jumped violently. They turned and saw

64

a tall man. He had come silently along the passage and had appeared without their noticing him.

They said nothing at all, but just stared at him. 'Come out here,' said the manager. They got up from their seats and went over to him. He took them each by the arm and marched them into the passage, along it for some way and then into his office. He sat down in his desk, his face stern.

'What are you doing in those seats?' he said. 'You haven't paid.'

'Yes, we have,' said Tom. 'We — we went to those seats because we like them.'

'This picture is an "Adults Only" one,' said the manager. 'You can only see it if some adult is with you. Who brought you in?'

This was too much for Bob. 'Nobody, sir! We came in by ourselves. We didn't know it was an adult picture.'

'*Did* you pay? Or did you sneak in by that door at the back?' asked the manager. 'Tell me the truth.'

Tom made a great mistake. The manager meant to scold them and let them off if they owned up — but Tom told a lie again.

'We paid,' he said. 'Didn't we, Bob?' And Bob, not liking to let Tom down, nodded his head. 'Yes,' he said. 'We both paid.'

CHAPTER TEN

## Trouble

That one, stupid lie was the beginning of a lot of trouble. The manager looked grim.

'Well, it's a pity you didn't own up,' he said. 'I'd

have let you off with a scolding for being a couple of stupid little idiots. But if you're going to lie about it too, that's another thing. What are your names and addresses?'

Now the two boys were frightened. Bob blurted out a few hurried words.

'We didn't pay! We're sorry, sir!'

'Too late now,' said the manager. 'Now – your names, please.'

The boys gave them, and also they had to give the name of their school. 'I think your Headmaster will have to know of this too,' said the manager. Bob and Tom felt aghast. Why had they been such idiots as to creep in without paying?

They went home in silence, and parted at Tom's front gate. 'Sorry I let you in for this,' said Tom. 'I hope you won't have too bad a time with your mother.'

Both boys had a very bad time indeed, not only with their parents, but with the Headmaster as well. He was shocked that two of his boys should do such a thing. He gave Bob a caning, and Tom got one from his father. But his mother's lamentations and scoldings were far worse than the caning! And the hard words from Bob's mother were worse to bear, too, than the Head's sharp strokes.

To add to their troubles they were made to pay the cinema for the tickets they should have bought. As Bob had only 10p and Tom had a 5p piece this wasn't enough. So it was decreed that they should both go without pocket-money for six weeks.

This was hard on Bob, because he had meant to buy Pat a nice birthday present. Now he couldn't buy one. He debated what to do. He rummaged through his belongings, but there was nothing a little girl would like. So he had to be content with making her a coloured card.

The Mackenzies had not been told anything about the escapade of the two boys. The parents had all been ashamed of it, and had told no one. The Head, of course, had said nothing. The only thing that the Mackenzies noticed was that Bob and Tom walked apart on the way to school, on the order of their parents, yet seemed extremely close friends at school. This was puzzling, but neither Tom nor Bob explained it.

The Berkeleys and Bob had all been asked to Pat's birthday party. Pat was very excited. She had seen her mother making her a big birthday cake – a sponge one with cream and chocolate filling, Pat's favourite. She had watched it being iced. She had delighted in the eight coloured candles set around it in sugar roses.

'It's lovely!' she told her mother. 'Much much better than a shop one. Fancy, I'll be eight. I shall feel much bigger.'

She wondered what Bob would give her. Before he had been punished by having to give up his pocket-money, he had been very mysterious about her birthday.

'You wait till you see what I'm going to get you!' he had said. 'Something you badly want. You just wait! I shall save up my money for it.'

And now there was no money to save up, and he couldn't even tell Pat why. Bob didn't want to spread the story of his escapade any more than his mother did.

The day of the party came. Twelve children trooped in at the gate: three Berkeleys, one Kent, and eight more school friends. Pat was there to greet them all, looking like a dark-haired pixie in a frilly pink frock.

Everyone brought her a present – except Bob. Even Tom had brought her one, having borrowed the money from Eleanor. Pat was delighted to undo the little parcels and see what was inside. Bob saw her undoing them, her cheeks crimson with excitement. He hated having nothing for her!

Pat was bitterly disappointed when Bob gave her only a card. Why had he said he was saving up and buying her something lovely? She liked him best of all − but he was the only one that hadn't brought her a present! The little girl stared at him in disappointment, and Bob felt ashamed.

He said the first thing that came into his head. 'I'm saving up to get you an extra-special thing at Christmas,' he said. 'A birthday-and-Christmas present put together − a doll that shuts its eyes!'

Pat was quite happy again. She squeezed Bob's arm. 'Oh − you *are* kind! Not one of my dolls shuts its eyes. I'd *rather* have one big present than two little ones! And thank you for the lovely card you made me, Bob.'

It was a jolly party, though the crowd in the two little rooms was rather too much. Still, nobody minded, and everyone enjoyed themselves − especially the Berkeleys and Bob, who always loved coming to the Mackenzies.

'What a lovely cake!' said Hilda, when she saw the big pink and white iced cake on the table, and watched the candles being lighted. 'Best I've ever seen!'

'I bet it tastes good too!'

Eleanor wished she could have a cake like that for *her* birthday. Birthdays weren't like this at home! Things always seemed such a burden to her mother. But Mrs Mackenzie didn't seem to mind anything. She sat at the head of the table and beamed away at everyone.

That was the last jollity that the Berkeleys and Bob had for some time. Things suddenly happened that were most unpleasant.

The first thing that happened was to Bob. His mother

suddenly announced to him that she had been accepted for the post she had applied for, and she was starting work the following Monday. Bob went pale. He had been hoping against hope that this wouldn't happen.

'Don't look so miserable!' said his mother. 'I told you about it before. You won't notice much difference, anyway, because you're used to staying at school for your dinner now.'

'Where is the job you're going to?' asked Bob, in a small voice. 'And what is it?'

'It's a job in a Beauty Shop,' said his mother. 'You have to have nice hair and nice hands and a good complexion to get the job, and I've got all those. It will do me good to get out and about and have a good job that pays good money.'

'Where is it?' said Bob again.

'It's in Hightown,' said his mother, and Bob's face fell. Hightown was a good way away. It would take his mother some time to get there and back.

'I shall have to leave before you go to school,' said Mrs Kent, 'but not long before. You can take the back door key with you, because I shan't be back to get you your tea. I'll leave it ready for you.'

'I can get it myself,' said Bob, in a curious muffled voice. 'Mum — have you *got* to take this job? I do so hate it. I don't want to come home when you're not here.'

'Now don't be selfish, Bob,' said his mother. 'It will make a lot of difference to us if I earn a bit of money. And I haven't noticed that you want to please me very much, or care about my feelings. Think of that dreadful cinema affair! I was never so ashamed in my life!'

Bob scowled. Why did his mother remind him of that so often! He wanted to forget it! He looked hard at his mother. He saw that it wasn't a bit of good trying to make her change her mind. Just as she had made up her mind to make him have his dinner at school, so now she had made up her mind to take this job. Bob had a miserable feeling that she didn't care for him at all!

He hung around his mother all the week-end, trying to think of something to say that would make her miraculously change her mind at the last minute. But the miracle didn't happen.

Monday morning came. Mrs Kent was up early bustling about. She got her breakfast and Bob's. She didn't light the fire, because there would be nobody in the house all day. The sitting-room was cold and cheerless.

Bob said nothing at all at breakfast. His mother felt half-cross and half-upset to see him looking so dismal. But he would soon get used to her going out to work, she comforted herself. Heaps of mothers worked these days. Why shouldn't she?

'Lock the back door when you go, and take the key,' his mother said. 'I've left the things in the larder for your tea. And here are your sandwiches ready for lunch. If you like to be useful when you get home, light the sitting-room fire for me!'

She smiled brightly at him, and went to put on her hat and coat. Then she came running through the hall. 'I must rush! I'll never catch the train! Good bye, Bob, cheer up!'

She made as if to kiss him but Bob turned away. She gave a little laugh. 'All right, sulky! Now don't get up to any mischief!'

The front door slammed. She was gone. The house suddenly seemed silent and empty and cheerless. Bob sat and stared at the breakfast things. Who was supposed to wash them up? He was, he supposed! And he was to come home and get his own tea, and light the fire

– and was he supposed to make his own bed? And who would do the dusting? Would his mother do it when she came home. All kinds of small problems crowded into Bob's muddled mind.

The clock struck nine o'clock. Fortunately it was a quarter of an hour fast. Bob leapt to his feet. He'd be late for school if he wasn't careful. Blow the breakfast things! Let them stay there unwashed. He couldn't bear this house one moment more without his mother!

He rushed to get his cap and coat and sandwiches. He went out of the back door and shut it and locked it behind him. He put the key into his pocket and ran down the path. He didn't look back at the horrid empty house.

He was difficult and awkward that day at school. He was either rude or had fits of showing off. Miss Roland looked at him in surprise. *Now* what was the matter? Bob had brains, he could work well, he was a good-tempered fellow on the whole – and yet he had these queer moody attacks when his whole nature seemed to alter.

'I shall really have to send you to the Headmaster, Bob,' she said at last. 'I've been as patient as possible, but the next time I have to speak to you, you'll have to go to the Head!'

That pulled Bob together a little. He wasn't very anxious to go to the Head. The last time he had had a word with him, he had been caned for the cinema affair. Bob didn't want to see the Head at all!

## CHAPTER ELEVEN

## *At Hawthorns and Summerhayes*

Bob went home slowly that afternoon. It was almost dark. The Mackenzies went with him, Pat chattering until she found him so silent that she too stopped talking. She looked at him timidly.

'Is anything the matter?' she asked. 'You tell me, Bob.'

'No, nothing,' said Bob, trying to speak lightly. 'I've got a bit of a headache, that's all.'

'Come in and have tea with us,' said Jeanie. Bob hesitated. He would have loved that. The thought of the Mackenzies' warm, bright home tempted him. Then he shook his head.

'No. I must get back. Got a lot to do! See you tomorrow, Mackenzies!'

He left them at their gate and went on to Hawthorns. It stood silent and dark, and no smoke came from its chimney. Bob hated the look of it. It should have had lights shining from it, the glow of a fire, smoke from the chimney, and cheerful sounds when he opened the door.

He unlocked the kitchen door. He felt something lick his hand as he did so, and jumped. But it was only Frisky! Frisky often came round to see if there were any tit-bits. Bob had never been so pleased to see a dog in his life. To Frisky's surprise he was dragged inside the kitchen and the door was shut behind him. Bob began to talk to him in a very loud, cheerful voice, and patted him. Frisky wagged his tail.

'You just stay here with me, Frisky,' said Bob, 'and

see what I get you! You can't think how pleased I am to have you. Look at this horrible cold dark house – it's empty. Nobody's here but you and me!'

'Wuff,' said Frisky, agreeing.

'My mother's gone out to work, Frisky,' said Bob. 'She doesn't care at all about *me*. What do you think of that, Frisky? She goes off before I leave for school, and she's not here when I come back. There's a lovely home for you, Frisky!'

Frisky looked puzzled. There was something unusual about Bob's voice that he didn't understand – but he was quite sure that Bob wasn't as cheerful as he sounded. He licked the boy's hand again.

Bob sat down on a chair and put his arms round Frisky's neck. 'I won't tell anyone but you,' he said, 'but I've got to tell someone or burst. You listen to this, Frisky. I'll tell you something dreadful. Well – I don't believe my mother loves me! And she's the only person I've got.'

He put his head against Frisky's neck and held the dog so tightly that Frisky whined. 'No, don't try to get away, Frisky,' said Bob. 'Just listen a bit. I'm in a muddle. Can you love someone and hate them too? I want to do kind things for my mother, and I want to pay her out for things as well. That's silly, isn't it, Frisky? Don't you think so?'

Frisky wriggled away. This boy was unhappy, Frisky knew that, but he didn't see why he should be strangled. He licked the boy's hands and then licked the tears on his cheeks. He put a big paw on Bob's knee and whined.

'Are you asking to go home?' said Bob, at last. He got up and opened the kitchen door. 'There you are. And thanks for listening to me, Frisky.'

But Frisky did not go. Frisky stayed, and that made

Bob feel happier. Bob washed up the breakfast things and laid the table for tea. He lighted the sitting-room fire. But it seemed a long, long time before his mother came home at half-past six. He was almost beside himself with worry when he heard the key of the front door put into the lock.

He rushed to greet her, all his resentment forgotten in his relief. But Frisky got there first and jumped up at her. She gave a squeal of fright and then pushed the dog away.

'Oh!' she said. 'It's Frisky. Whatever have you got him here for, Bob? You know I don't like him in the house. It's too bad of you, when I come home tired, to have a great dog like Frisky messing round!'

'I'll take him back,' said Bob, bitterly disappointed with his mother, all his joy at seeing her fading away. He took Frisky by the collar and led him out. He took him right to the back door of Barlings, opened it quietly and let him in. Then he crept round to the front of the house and peeped through a crack of the curtains into the lighted sitting-room there.

He saw what he expected to see. The whole family was there. Mr Mackenzie was sitting in his chair smoking his pipe, with Pat on his knee telling him something. Mrs Mackenzie was darning, listening to something that Jeanie was telling her. Jeanie was drawing at the same time, and near her was Donald doing his homework.

The fire burnt cheerfully. The cat sat in front of it, its tail curled neatly round. Frisky suddenly bounded in and made a great fuss of everyone.

Bob drank it all in as if his mind was thirsty for what he saw. Then he turned away, envy in his heart. Donald and Jeanie took all that for granted. They didn't know how lucky they were! Bob kicked his way back to Hawthorns, looking sullen.

And at Summerhayes also something was happening that made an upheaval in the household there. Mr Berkeley had gone!

He had been quiet and listless for the last day or two, and had left undone many of the things his wife liked him to do. She had nagged at him as usual, and then one of the usual rows had flared up, all in front of the three children. The girls began to cry, and Tom stood up to go out of the room in disgust. But something his father had said made him stop.

He spoke in a quiet voice. 'This is the end. It's not good for any of us to go on like this. I am sure that you are right when you say that I am to blame for everything. So I'm going. Then perhaps you will be happier, all of you.'

He left the room without another word, brushing by Tom. He went upstairs and they heard him opening drawers and cupboards. Eleanor tore upstairs too.

'Dad! What are you doing? Don't go! I don't want you to go!'

Her father said nothing, but clipped shut his big suitcase. He didn't even look at Eleanor. She shrank back from his stern white face. He looked suddenly much older.

The front door slammed. The front gate clicked shut. Quick footsteps went down the lane, and then faded away.

'He's gone!' wailed Hilda. 'I don't want him to go.'

'He'll come back,' said her mother, dabbing her eyes. 'He did before.'

But Mr Berkeley didn't come back. No one put a key in the front door that night and crept upstairs. No one slept in the bed in the little dressing room. Mr Berkely *didn't* come back!

That was a dreadful time for the three children. They

had to cope with a tearful, complaining, angry mother, who had no idea where her husband was. They had to promise her not to tell anyone their father had gone away because of a row. They were to say he was on a visit. They had to face the fact that perhaps their father might never come back again.

'I couldn't bear that,' said Hilda, wiping her eyes. 'Daddy wasn't so bad as Mother always made out. She made him miserable.'

'We all made him miserable,' said Eleanor. 'We were all miserable, really. All that bickering and quarrelling! Dad's well out of it.'

'I hope Mother doesn't turn on *us* now and nag at us too much,' said Tom, fearfully. 'I got a pretty bad time of it over that cinema affair.'

'Well, you deserved it,' said Eleanor. 'That was a shocking thing to do.'

'Now don't *you* start nagging!' said Tom, desperately. 'We've got trouble enough without that!'

'We're a beastly family,' said Hilda. 'A very — beastly — family. I wish Dad hadn't gone. I wasn't very nice to him, but it's going to be awful without a father.'

It certainly *was* awful! They missed him much more than they had ever dreamed they would. They kept asking their mother where he was, and if he was coming back.

She was very subdued one day. She had had a letter, a serious letter. 'He's made up his mind not to come back,' she said. 'He's sending us money every month. Oh, why has this happened to me?'

All three children could have told her; but they said nothing. They stood there, looking profoundly dismayed. They felt as if their home was breaking up.

Mrs Berkeley looked upon herself as a poor, badly-treated woman. She longed to tell someone, so she went in one day to open her heart to Mrs Mackenzie.

But Mrs Mackenzie proved surprisingly unsym-
pathetic. 'Andy, my husband, says you had a good
man and a kind one,' she said. 'He helped willingly
with the properties for the school play. I liked him
too. There was nothing wrong with him that I could
see, Mrs Berkeley.'

'Oh, but you don't know the dreadful things he said
to me,' said Mrs Berkeley, beginning to cry.

'No, and I don't want to know them,' said Mrs
Mackenzie firmly. 'There are always faults on both
sides, and your biggest fault, both of you, is that you
only think of yourselves and not of the children. Poor
things, going about with anxious looks, pretending their
father's gone on a visit! Can't you see what you're
doing to those children of yours?'

'You're unkind,' wept Mrs Berkeley. 'I wish I hadn't
come to you for advice.'

'Ah well, if it's advice you're needing I'll give it
to you,' said Mrs Mackenzie. 'Now you listen to me.
You write to that husband of yours and tell him you're
downright sorry for all you've said and done, tell him
you're missing him and the children are too; tell him
you'll turn over a new leaf for their sake, if only he'll
come back.'

'Oh, I couldn't possibly do that!' said Mrs Berkeley,
horrified. 'I'm not in the wrong. He's always been the
one to fail us.'

'Maybe he thinks the same of you,' said Mrs
Mackenzie, dryly. 'But while you can do without your
husband if it suits you, your children can't do without
a father – especially that boy of yours, Tom. A fine
boy he is, but all fine boys need a father's hand. Get
your man back before things go worse for you!'

'I can manage my family all right, thank you,' said
Mrs Berkeley, rising with a very dignified air, and

dabbing her eyes. 'I'm sorry to have come in and troubled you. I'll not bother you again.'

And out she sailed, her head in the air. She would show Mrs Mackenzie she could run her family all right without begging their father to come back!


CHAPTER TWELVE

## Bob in a Rage

And now began a miserable time for the children at Summerhayes and Hawthorns. A time that was to have a lasting effect on them all, the marks of which would never quite wear off.

Eleanor and Hilda were very unhappy, for three reasons. They missed their father; they hated having to pretend he was coming back at any moment; and their mother was so harassed and felt herself to be such a martyr that there was even less peace and comfort in their home that there had been before.

But it was the two boys that felt the anxiety the most – Bob, at Hawthorns, with his mother always out, and Tom at Summerhayes trying to rid himself of the load that his mother continually put on his shoulders.

The conditions at home drove the two boys together more and more. They became very fast friends indeed. It was a comfort to Bob to feel that he had a friend bigger and older than himself, who admired him and talked to him and confided in him. It was a relief to Tom to have someone to grumble to and unload his worry on. Bob would listen for half an hour at a time if Tom wanted to tell him anything.

Bob hadn't got used to his mother's going out to work. He hated her leaving before him in the morning. He hated even more having to come back to an empty house at night. Mrs Mackenzie had learnt by now that Mrs Kent went out to work, and she had Bob in whenever she could.

'To leave that boy to come home to a cold empty house and no tea is a wicked thing to do!' she told her husband. 'He's got no father – and now he's no mother to speak of.'

'He's a good boy too,' said her husband. 'Look how he came in every evening and read to Pat when she had the 'flu last week. He made the child as happy as a blackbird!'

'And the things he does for me!' said Mrs Mackenzie. 'You wouldn't believe it, Andy. I've got to stop him doing some of them because Donald got quite jealous! He's a fine boy wasted, is Bob. His father would have been proud of him.'

Bob noticed the great difference in his mother as the days went by. She looked younger and prettier as she learnt ways to beautify herself. She bought herself gay clothes, and looked bright and cheerful. She enjoyed her new life.

Bob was the only thing that spoilt her pleasure. He too had changed. He was no longer the loving, noisy, merry boy he once had been. He was silent and moody, resentful and unhelpful. He no longer washed up the breakfast things or lighted the fire for her. He hardly listened when she told him the little things that had happened in her day.

'I'm bringing a friend home,' she told him one evening. 'It's the woman who works with me. Will you try to get the fire lighted, Bob, and wash up the breakfast things, and set the tea? We'll be back about half-past five – I think I can be early tomorrow.'

Bob grunted. She said no more, but sighed. How difficult he was! Perhaps if she gave him a nice little sum of pocket money he would act better?

'Here, Bob,' she said, getting out her purse. 'Here's 25p for you. Buy yourself something nice.'

Bob looked coldly at the money. 'I haven't finished paying that cinema manager for the ticket I didn't buy,' he said. 'Have you forgotten? I'm not supposed to have any money till I've paid for it out of the 10p a week you give me.'

Mrs Kent had forgotten. 'Never mind,' she said, pushing the money over. 'Take this. Perhaps it will bring a smile to your face!'

Bob pushed the money away so roughly that it clattered to the ground. 'I don't want any money you earn!' he said in a trembling voice. 'I'd rather have you here at home, where you belong. I don't feel as if I've *got* a home now. I hate coming in after school. Sometimes I feel I could smash the whole place up!'

'Bob!' said his mother, really shocked. 'Now just listen while I explain how much nicer it is for me to . . .'

'I don't want to hear,' said Bob, and he got up to go out of the room. 'You like your job better than you like me. That's all I know!'

He went out. Mrs Kent looked into the fire, worried. She *couldn't* give up her job now. She liked the people she worked with, she liked the bustle and laughter, she liked the money she got – though she confessed to herself that she really didn't need that! She looked at herself in the glass. She was quite pretty now that she knew how to make herself nice. She felt her soft hands and smoothed her face. What a pity Bob wasn't proud of her looks, and didn't give her admiration and love as he used to do! Whatever had come over him lately?

Something certainly came over Bob the next day. He came home from school to the usual empty, cold, cheerless house, remembering that he had to get things ready for his mother and her friend.

He stared moodily at the ashes in the hearth that he must clear before he lighted the fire, and at the unwashed breakfast things with hard grease on the plates. He looked at the kettle on the stove, and the undrawn curtains left pulled back from the morning.

And suddenly something snapped, and temper flared up in him. He hated the fire and the breakfast things and the kettle and everything else! He hated the room and the house. He kicked the mat, and that started it.

He hurled the breakfast crockery across the room and laughed when it broke into pieces. He took the kettle from the stove and threw that at the wall. It broke a picture. He kicked all the mats up, and put his hands in the dead ashes, scattering them all over the place. What a mess!

He stood staring at what he had done. He felt better for doing all that, though he knew it was mad and silly and wrong. He turned and went out of the house and made his way to the Mackenzies'. They gave him a great welcome.

His mother was horrified when she went into Hawthorns with her friend. It was in darkness, and there was no smoke coming from the chimney. What had happened to Bob?

She switched on the light in the sitting-room and stared in fright. Who had done all this? Who had smashed the china, broken the picture — and surely that wasn't the *kettle* lying on its side in the corner? And what was this grey ash all over the place? She was bewildered and angry.

Could it have been *Bob*? No, he couldn't do a thing

like that to her! It was impossible. She and her friend cleared up the room. She lighted the fire, and put the kettle on to boil. Things were soon fairly straight again, but Mrs Kent couldn't feel straight herself. It was all so odd – and how could she explain to her friend? She felt ashamed. If all this *was* caused by Bob she would have something to say to him!

After her friend had gone. Mrs Kent made a search for Bob in the house, in case he had hidden himself away, but he wasn't to be found. She thought he might be at the Mackenzies', and went to find out.

Yes, there he was, said Mrs Mackenzie. He had been helping Mr Mackenzie with a ship he was making. 'You come along in for a minute, Mrs Kent,' she said. But Mrs Kent shook her head.

'Just tell Bob I want him to come home with me at once,' she said. And in a moment or two Bob appeared, said thank you and good-night to Mrs Mackenzie, and walked back silently to Hawthorns with his mother.

As soon as they were in the sitting-room she turned to him. 'Bob! Did *you* leave all that mess about?' she demanded.

'What mess?' asked Bob.

'You know quite well what I mean!' she cried. 'The broken cups and plates – the ashes all over the place, the . . .'

'Oh *that*,' said Bob, as if it was all nothing. 'Yes, I did that. I just had to. I might do it again, if I get that feeling.'

His mother stared at him. 'Bob! You seem so strange – talking like that about the awful thing you did. Think what I felt when I came in with my friend and saw all that!'

'I'm glad!' said Bob. 'I didn't want her to come. Why should she come here and find the fire lighted and tea

83

ready and everything – and when I come home there's nothing?'

Mrs Kent argued with him, but he wouldn't budge from his reasons, nor would he say he was sorry. 'It's like arguing with a stone wall!' she said at last, almost in tears. 'You're a horrid unkind boy, and if you think that kind of thing will make me love you, you're mistaken. It will only make me dislike you.'

'You don't care anything about me at all,' said Bob. 'I'm just a nuisance now – or someone who can get things ready for you. I'm a nuisance when you're home for the week-ends and you want me out of the way when you get the house cleaned. I'm a nuisance in the evenings when you want to go out to the cinema. Well, nuisances break things up, and that's what I did!'

His mother looked at him standing there defying her. He was only ten – not even a big boy yet! How could he say such awful things? She didn't deserve it, she thought, and she began to cry.

Bob remembered how Tom had said that his own mother always cried when she felt herself defeated and yet wanted her own way still. He hardened his heart and turned away, feeling suddenly much older than his years.

'I warn you, Mum – I might break things again,' he said, not really meaning it, but just to punish her and frighten her, and stop her from bringing her friend home and expecting things to be nice for them.

'You cruel boy!' said Mrs Kent. 'If that's the kind of thing you're going to do when I'm out, I shall see that you leave for school before I go, and I shall lock all the doors behind me! You'll have to wait till I get home before you come in!'

'I don't mind,' said Bob. 'I'd rather do that than come into an empty house. I'd wait willingly till you come home – it will be nice to find a fire and a light when I open the door, instead of darkness and coldness.'

And that was how it was that Mrs Kent locked up the house before she left, so that Bob had to wait outside by himself each evening, cold and hungry and tired.

CHAPTER THIRTEEN

## The Gang

Down in the town there was a little gang of boys. The youngest was eight, the oldest was fifteen. There were four of them, Len, Jack, Patrick, a wild Irish boy, and Fred. They met each evening, and every Saturday and Sunday; their favourite playground was a terrace of half-ruined old houses that were to be pulled down.

Under one of these houses was a cellar. The four boys had found it by accident one day, and were delighted.

'Coo! Look here,' said Len, peering down some stone steps. 'What's this? Underground tunnel or something? Let's play spies! This would be a fine hiding place!'

It certainly was! Down the stone steps was a small dark stone cellar. The walls were damp, and the place smelt musty and bad. But the boys didn't mind. It was a hidey-hole, a place where nobody could find them.

Jack thought of the idea of making it a proper meeting place, and proposed that they should try and furnish it in some way.

'We could get a few boxes, see?' he said. 'And what about pinching a bit of old carpet from somewhere? And we could get a candle from home. My mum would give me one.'

This hidey-hole was one of the greatest pleasures of the little gang. To it they brought their treasures: an old pack of cards, dirty and sticky, Len's little clockwork engine, some comics, a broken candlestick for the candle – and, the oddest thing of all, a toy telephone!

This was brought by Fred, the eldest boy. He was very proud of it indeed. He had seen it in a toy-shop and had 'pinched' it – stolen it when the shop was fairly full and nobody had been looking.

He had seen rich men at the cinema with telephones crowding their desks, and although he himself had never used a telephone it seemed to him that it was a sign of power and of riches. He must have one too, even though it was only a toy one.

So there stood this little telephone on a box, and the other three boys used to listen with bated breath while Fred talked down it, giving orders to mythical spies or gangsters in an American voice!

Sometimes they brought food down there and shared it. They planned raids on this garden and that when fruit was in season. They thought out silly tricks, such as knocking on doors and then running away.

Len was the youngest, and his brother was Fred, the fifteen-year-old. Jack was eleven, Patrick was twelve, loud-voiced, fiery-tempered, amusing and cunning.

Len and Fred had no father. They ran completely wild. Their mother didn't bother about them in the least. They cheeked her, took money from her purse when she left it about, and were quite out of control.

Patrick had no mother, only a father who had no time for him, but beat him regularly 'just to keep him in order', so he said. Patrick hated his father and kept away from him as much as he could.

Jack had both mother *and* father, and two brothers

and three sisters. But as they all lived together in two rooms the boy escaped from home as much as he could. The two rooms were dirty and smelly and untidy. No one could eat, sleep or read in comfort. Jack hated his home, and though he really loved his mother he couldn't bear her whining voice and miserable face. Poor woman, she had long ago given up all hope of getting a place big enough for her large family, and had lost heart. It was no wonder the boy went to find happiness somewhere else – and to him the little hidey-hole down in the cellar was heaven.

None of the boys was very clever. Patrick had a streak of cunning that the gang found useful, but they had a healthy respect for the two policeman of that district, and kept out of their way as much as possible.

'We're the Four Terrors Gang,' Fred had announced one night. 'We aren't afraid of the coppers or anybody, and don't you forget it.'

'We aren't afraid of nobody!' said Patrick. It wasn't true, of course. They were afraid of their teachers, the 'coppers', one or two shopkeepers who shouted at them – and Patrick was terribly afraid of his father. But they liked pretending they were quite fearless. For a little while they felt grand and on top of the world!

Fred picked up the receiver of the toy telephone, and at once his three 'men' were respectfully silent. They listened eagerly. Fred was grand on the telephone.

'Is that Number 61045?' said Fred, in the short sharp voice he used at times. 'This is the Chief here – chief of the Four Terrors. Here's my orders. You'll take five men with you and the big car, and you'll go to Scarface and get his orders – then you'll . . .'

The one-sided conversation would go on for about two minutes. Then Fred would put down the little receiver and say, 'Well, that's settled, boys. The men are on the job!'

The gang always wanted money – money to buy food, money to go to the pictures, which they loved above anything else. To sit in a comfortable seat in a warm place and see people being chased and shot, to see horses galloping at top speed, cars tearing along at eighty miles an hour, aeroplanes being revved up . . . this was all glorious to them. They didn't have to think, or use their brains at all – they only needed to sit back and look.

It was into this gang that Bob stumbled one night. It was about a week after his mother had begun to take the keys of the house with her, so that he couldn't get in till she came back at half-past six. She left him some cake on a shelf in their little garden shed, but he never touched it.

'Leaving out food for me as if I was the cat next door!' he grumbled to himself. 'I'll wait till she comes home, and have supper – proper supper, even if she has to cook it when she's tired.'

But it was difficult to fill in the time between afternoon school and half-past six. The evenings were quite dark now, and cold.

'You can always go into the Mackenzies',' his mother said to Bob. 'They'll be pleased to have you, goodness knows why!'

But Bob didn't go. He was ashamed to have to say that he couldn't get into his own house. He only went once, when they asked him to come to tea and help with something they were making. He worked so hard and well that Mr Mackenzie was amazed.

'Come again,' he said. 'You're good with your hands. You've done twice as much as old Donald here! Come in any time you can. I want to get this finished for Christmas.'

Most nights Bob wandered down into the town by himself. He kicked his way along moodily, his school satchel on his back. He stared into any shops that were open, and into any lighted living-rooms. Families had a kind of obsession for him.

One night it was pouring with rain. Bob was down in the town. He wondered if he should go home and sit in the shed – or should he go to the Mackenzies? No, he wouldn't. He'd find shelter somewhere.

He came to where some houses were half-tumbled-down. 'I'll shelter here,' he thought, and scrambled over fallen bricks to find a corner of a ruined room.

And then he suddenly heard a voice coming from below him – a short, staccato voice, issuing orders. Bob stood in astonishment.

'Hallo! That Number 678345? This is the Chief speaking. What do you mean by not coming along when I told you? Here we've been waiting an hour or more! You afraid of being ticked off for failing in that job you had to do? Well, you know what happens to men who're yellow! Unless you come along straight away, look out for trouble! The Four Terrors will be after you!'

Bob was simply amazed. What was this? Who was speaking like that, just below him?

Then he saw a dim light somewhere down below. He bent down and saw that he was near some stone steps that led underground. He felt excited. What was all this. Had he discovered some secret hiding-place?

He cautiously put one foot on the top step. Then down another step, and another. The rain pelted down all the time, making a great noise, so that it hid the sound of his feet on the rubbly stone steps.

He came in view of the cellar, and stared in astonishment. He saw a little square place with damp walls. Boxes here and there, and an old piece of damp carpet

was on the floor. A big box stood in the middle for a table, and in it was a pile of comics and a candle set in a ginger-beer bottle. On another box stood a telephone – the little toy telephone that Fred was so proud of.

Four boys sat in the candle-lighted cellar. All were reading comics. They hardly ever read anything else. Bob stood and stared: it looked so cosy and exciting and most surprising to him.

Patrick suddenly looked up and saw him. He shouted. 'Hey! Look there! Who's that?'

Then Bob had a real brain-wave. He grinned widely and said:

'I'm Number 678345! You telephoned me just now. I've come along to report to the Chief.'

There was dead silence in the cellar. All four boys stared at Bob, extremely startled by what he had said.

Who was he? How did he know anything about them? Had he really 'come to report'?

Fred rose to the occasion. He had sized Bob up at once – a boy a bit above them in station, a daredevil, someone with a sense of humour. He might be useful!

'Come in, Number 678345,' he said. 'Good thing you came along! I was just going to send someone for you!'

Bob went right into the cellar. Fred took his precious telephone off its box, and pushed the box over to Bob for a seat. 'I suppose you heard me telephoning,' he said.

'Yes,' said Bob. 'I couldn't make it out! Were you *really* telephoning with that telephone?'

Fred didn't answer. He sometimes almost persuaded himself that he really *was* telephoning to distant members of the gang, and he didn't want to admit that he wasn't. He lived in a curious world of make-believe.

'It's pouring,' said Bob. 'Do you mind if I shelter here for a bit? I like this place. Cosy, isn't it — a home from home!'

'Stay as long as you like,' said Fred. 'We're all pals together here!'

## CHAPTER FOURTEEN

## A 'Home from Home'

The Four Terrors all took to Bob at once. He showed off rather, talked big, and was very friendly. His obvious pleasure in their curious hidey-hole pleased them.

'Come again, pal,' said Fred when he went. 'You're welcome any time. There's always a comic to spare!'

So Bob went again — and yet again. The little dimly-lighted cellar had a peculiar fascination for him. He felt safe there, and he felt welcome. All four boys admired him and liked him, and because he was better-dressed than they were and came from a better home they were proud to have him share their cellar.

'It's cold in here,' said Bob one night. 'Why don't we have a fire?'

'We can't,' said Patrick. 'We tried it once — brought some wood down that we pinched from a wood-pile. But it almost smoked us out! We've got no chimney, you see.'

'What about an oil stove?' said Bob. 'That would be just the thing!'

'Garn! How are we to get an oil stove?' said Patrick, scornfully. 'They don't grow on trees.'

'I could bring one,' said Bob. 'I'll bring one tomorrow night. Patrick, you come along to my house and carry the oil for it. We'll have a can. Then we shall be warm and cosy.'

This was just about the most exciting thing that had happened to the gang. The only thing that had spoilt the hiding place was its dampness and coldness. Now they would be warm!

The oil stove was a tremendous success. It warmed the little cellar immediately, and the red glow it gave out was very pleasant. Patrick looked at Bob gratefully.

'Thanks,' he said. 'I'll have to take off my coat soon! Say, Fred – oughtn't we to make Bob a Terror too? Then we'd be Five Terrors.'

Fred looked round at the others. 'What do you say, men?' he asked, solemnly. Patrick, Jack, and Len put up their hands at once, almost as if they were in school.

'I say yes,' said Jack, and the others said the same. Fred turned to Bob.

'Shake!' he said, and held out a very dirty hand to Bob. Bob was thrilled. Now he was really accepted by this gang! He had belonged to a very harmless gang of small boys in Croydon – this one was much more the real thing! He shook hands solemnly with Fred, Patrick, Jack and Len.

It was a pleasant evening indeed, because Bob had not only brought the oil stove but the cake his mother had left in the shed for him. So the boys munched happily, felt warm and read their everlasting comics. They were sorry to have to get up and go home.

It was late when Bob got back – half past eight! His mother was worried and cross.

'Where have you been? I won't have you staying out like this. I've been to Bill's,' said Bob, untruthfully. It was so much easier to tell a lie than to have arguments and scoldings. Anyway he couldn't possibly say he had been with the gang. He couldn't give them away!

Bob took an old rug down to the little cellar the next night. Then he took a small table. He took glasses to drink from, and another bottle of orangeade from his mother's cupboard. Another night he took a meat pie from the larder, and the gang had a wonderful feast.

There was an argument about the meat pie, and his mother was very cross about it. 'When did you take it? And why? You couldn't have eaten it all yourself!'

'I took it this morning and put it in the shed ready for when I got home at night,' said Bob, which was true. 'I ate it all myself.' Which was untrue.

'You're getting to be a very naughty, difficult boy,' scolded his mother. 'I shall have to lock the larder door now!'

The gang thought that Bob was a wonderful member of the Five Terrors. They never knew what he was going to bring next to the little cellar. It really was beginning to look very homely and cosy.

Bob had raided the loft in the roof of Hawthorn Cottage. He had found plenty of things there that would do for the cellar — and old kettle to boil water on top of the oil stove, some cups and plates, two cushions and a small stool. He brought them all one by one in the darkness, first putting them out in the shed so that they would be ready for him to collect at night. He couldn't get into the house to take them then, of course, because the doors were locked.

'This is a real palace now,' said Jack, looking round, comparing it with the place he called home. 'I've got somewhere to keep my things safe now. At home there isn't even a corner I can have — my sisters and brothers take anything they can of mine!'

Each boy had a small part of the cellar to call his

own. There they kept their own precious little belongings, and not one of the Five would have dreamed of touching anyone else's things.

'I wonder your mother doesn't miss all the things you've pinched from her,' Fred said to Bob. 'You're a wonder at pinching, you are!'

'Taking things from my mother isn't pinching – I don't call *that* stealing,' said Bob, at once.

'Garn!' said Patrick. 'That's pinching all right! That's stealing! If the police caught you, and your mum said these things were hers down here, we'd all be taken off to the police station! But we're well hidden here – no one will ever find out!'

Just before Christmas Tom joined the gang too. His home was a most uncomfortable place now – his father had not come back, his mother whined and worried, and Tom had a great many jobs to do that he resented.

Hilda and Eleanor did what they could, but none of them had been taught to be unselfish or to pull together, and now that trouble had come to the household they didn't know how to tackle it.

Money was short and the girls couldn't have new party frocks. Tom couldn't have a new overcoat, and he was ashamed of his because he had grown lately – his wrists stuck out of the sleeves and looked ridiculous. He wished his father would come back.

'All these women round me!' he thought crossly, thinking of his mother and sisters. 'Always grousing and grumbling and whining! I wish I could clear out like Dad.'

He took to going out every evening to one or other of his friends' houses. One evening he went to Bob's house, but it was in darkness. Then he heard someone in the shed at the back. Was it Bob? What could he be doing?

He went to see. He saw Bob come out of the shed, carrying something. He followed him curiously without being heard. Bob went down the path and out of the gate. As he passed under the street lamp Tom saw that he was carrying three large cardboard boxes. It looked as if they were the boxes that his railway set was kept in.

'He's going to somebody's house to set it out,' thought Tom. 'I'll follow him and see whose it is. I'd like a game with that railway tonight, so perhaps I could go with him. He may be going to Harry's.'

But Bob didn't go to Harry's. He went to his usual place – the hidey-hole in the cellar. Tom was astonished when he followed Bob down to the town, and across to the old houses – and then Bob disappeared underground!

It didn't take long for Tom to discover the cellar. He went down the steps into the warm, candle-lit place. Five boys looked up at him, frozen stiff with fear. Who had found their hole? The police?

'TOM!' cried Bob, and leapt up so relieved that it wasn't the police or any grown-up that he gave his friend a far warmer welcome than he would have in the ordinary way. Tom looked round the cellar in amazement.

'Gosh! Is this where you come? What is it – a meeting place or something?'

'Who's he?' said Fred sharply to Bob. 'A friend of yours? How's he know about this?'

'I followed him,' explained Tom. 'All right, don't scowl at me like that. I won't give you away. You're a gang, I suppose? Bob, you never told me! This place is a wizard place, isn't it?'

The gang waited for Tom to go. They were prepared to put up with him for a few minutes – but this was their own place and they didn't want any visitors. Tom sensed their feelings.

'I won't stop,' he said. 'I'm not going to butt in, but I say, if you ever want another member who'll do his bit — and a big bit too — think of me, will you?'

'Can he stay?' asked Bob. 'I'm going to set out my railway for you all to see tonight, and Tom knows how to do it with me. He'd be useful.'

'Okay,' said Fred, rather reluctantly. He would have refused anyone else — but Bob was so very useful to the gang, and most of the comforts they had in their little room had been brought by him. It was difficult to say no to him.

So Tom stayed. The railway was put out, and the six boys had a fine time arranging collisions and accidents, working the signals and taking it in turn to wind up the engines. Even fifteen-year-old Fred was completely fascinated. It was late when they packed up.

'Gosh — half-past nine!' said Tom. 'I'm going to get into a row. Not that that's anything new. I bet you'll get into one too, Bob.'

'Fat lot I care!' said Bob. 'Only thing I want now is something to eat. I'll have to pinch something out of the larder when I get home, if my mother hasn't locked the door!'

Fred pulled Bob back as he was about to go up the stone steps after Tom. 'Say! Would you like to ask that friend of yours to be in the gang?' he whispered. 'He's a good bloke, isn't he? He's got brains too.'

'I'll ask him,' said Bob, delighted. It certainly *would* be nice to have Tom in the gang — they could go down together every night and come home together. Tom was always at a loose end — surely he'd love to come!

And so Tom too became a member of the gang.

The *Six* Terrors it was now, and the little cellar became rather crowded. But nobody minded that.

Tom added his bit to the gang – more oil for the stove, more candles, food, drink, another cushion. The boys thought it was the cosiest, finest place in the whole kingdom.

'It's really a *home*,' said Jack. 'That's what we've made it – a home!'

## CHAPTER FIFTEEN

## *Money for the Gang*

Tom made a difference to the gang. He was not so content as they were to sit in the cellar each evening and read comics. He brought some books down, but, except for Bob, not one of the others wanted to read a book.

'It's too difficult,' complained Patrick, throwing down a book that Tom had handed him. 'By the time I've spelt out a sentence I've forgotten the meaning. Comics are best – all pictures! If you don't want to read what's underneath, you needn't. You can tell by the pictures. I like comics best – and the cinema too. You don't have to think with either of them.'

'Well, what about going to the pictures tomorrow?' said Tom. 'All of us. There's a super picture on, called *He Killed Six*! Plenty of shooting, I bet.'

'Bang, bang, bang!' said Len, pretending to fire a gun. 'Wish I had a gun! I'd shoot plenty of people. Bang, bang, bang!'

'Shut up,' said Fred, who rarely allowed his small brother to enter into the conversation. ' 'Nuff said from you, young Len!' He turned to Tom. 'The trouble about going to the pictures, pal, is that tickets cost money. You never thought of that, I suppose?'

'Don't be funny,' said Tom. 'Who of us has got any money? You a rich man yet?'

'Here!' said Patrick, suddenly. 'I know a place where there's money, see?'

'Where?' asked Fred.

'You know that newsagent's round the corner where I live?' said Patrick. 'Well, the old man there keeps his money in a box on the shelf at the back of the shop. I've seen him put it there when I buy cigarettes for my Dad. He's a mean old man, that. He once gave me 5p too little in my change and Dad gave me a real beating when I got back.'

There was silence. Bob felt uncomfortable. What was Patrick proposing?

'Well, go on,' said Fred. 'Do you want to get your 5p back?'

'That's right,' said Patrick, nodding his head till his long, greasy hair fell over his face. 'If one of you can come with me to keep watch, I can climb in at a little window at the back. The old man would be upstairs out of the way by now.'

There was another silence.

'Gah!' said Patrick, in scorn. 'Lot of cowards, you are! Yellow, that's what you are! Daren't come and keep watch for me while I get a 5p that's my own!'

'I'll come,' said Tom, stung by the taunt. 'Who cares, anyway? I'd like a bit of excitement. I'll come, Patrick.'

'Better not, Tom,' said Bob.

'Don't take any notice of *him*!' said Patrick, scornfully. 'He only pinches form his ma! Nothing wrong in that, is there, Bob?'

Bob looked fierce, but Fred pushed Patrick away.

'Clear off and get your 5p,' he said. 'No fights here. You know that.'

Patrick went up the steps, followed by Tom. The other four waited uneasily. Suppose Patrick was caught?

But in twenty minutes' time there came the low whistle that was the gang's signal, and down came the two boys, swaggering and boasting.

'It was easy!' said Patrick. 'Easy as eating cake! I opened the window, slid in, went to the shelf at the back of the shop – and there you are!'

'A copper came along, and nearly spotted me,' said Tom, proudly. 'But I hid behind a dustbin and he went on. Patrick was as slippery as an eel. He went in at that window like a shadow.'

Everyone felt excited. This was an adventure. It was all very well to play and pretend they were spies or burglars, up against detectives or policemen – this was the real thing! Bob, Fred, Len and Jack looked at Patrick and Tom with great respect.

Pat jingled the money in his pocket and grinned. Fred looked at him sharply.

'Turn out your pockets!' he commanded. Patrick hesitated. 'Turn them out!' said Fred, angrily. 'You going to disobey me?'

Patrick emptied one of his pockets on to the little table. There were 50p, 10p, 5p and 1p coins!

'Were you going to keep that lot for yourself?' said Fred, fiercely. 'Share and share alike, that's what this gang does, see? I've a good mind to kick you all the way up those stairs!'

Tom stared at the money in surprise. 'Did you take all that from the old man's box?' he asked. 'I thought you went for your 5p.'

Patrick laughed. 'So I did, mate. But I took the rest for my trouble, see? Any objection?'

'You'd better take it back,' said Bob. He was troubled. This was robbery.

'Garn! Take it back yourself!' said Patrick. He looked round defiantly. 'Anyone want to take it back?' he asked. 'They're welcome to, if they want to. But I bet the old man's found out now and the police are there!'

There was a dead silence. Then Fred spoke up. 'Well, the money's here – and no one wants to take it back. Count it out, Patrick, and we'll share it. Keep an extra 5p for yourself.'

'I'm keeping,' said Patrick. 'I did the dirty work, didn't I? Tom can have an extra 5p for watching.'

'Don't want it,' said Tom. But he took it all the same, when the money was shared out. Bob was very silent. He didn't want to take his share, but he knew that it would cause a lot of sneering comment if he didn't. He put it into his pocket, making up his mind to take it home, put it in a safe place, and somehow get it back to the old man.

But he didn't. The very next day he heard that Pat had been taken to hospital with appendicitis. Jeanie and Donald told him the news as they walked to school.

'It was in the middle of the night,' said Jeanie, with a white face. 'The doctor came because Pat's tummy hurt her so – and he got an ambulance and took her away to hospital. She's had an operation to make her better.'

'Is she all right now?' asked Bob, anxiously. He was still very fond of Pat, and always talked to her on the way to school.

'Yes, she's quite all right, but she's got to stay there ten days,' said Donald. 'Mother says would you like to go and see her, Bob? She can see people tomorrow. You can take her a book to read if you like.'

'Or flowers,' said Jeanie. 'Our Pat loves flowers. Only they're so expensive now.'

'It was *awful* without Pat at breakfast,' said Donald. 'Simply awful! I felt dreadful too, because yesterday evening I wouldn't read to Pat when she asked me. I was busy with my fret-saw. Now I keep on and on worrying because I wouldn't do that for her. I'm going to see her every single day and take her a little present. Every single day.'

Bob had no money at all except the money from the gang. He had just finished paying for that wretched cinema ticket, and his Saturday 5p wasn't due yet. He wasn't going to ask his mother for money, either! Let her keep her earnings to herself, thought Bob, bitterly, his usual resentment flooding up when he thought of his mother.

He thought about Pat. He pictured her lying in a hospital bed, all alone, longing for her family to see her – longing for Bob to come too! Bob knew that. He knew that Pat loved him and was proud that he liked to be with her. She wasn't one-on-her-own when he was about.

'Did you say we could see her tomorrow?' he asked. 'What time? Oh, any time, good. I'll go after afternoon school, if that's all right. She's in a room by herself, you said, so I can stay a bit, can't I?'

'Yes, so long as you don't tire her,' said Jeanie. 'The nurse will tell you how long to stay.'

Bob thought about Pat a lot that day. He had told her he would be her brother and she was his little sister. He was sure he wanted her more than either Jeanie or Donald did. He remembered how she had slipped her small hand into his when she had the 'flu and he had read to her each night. She was a darling!

'If I had a sister like Pat I'd never have joined the Gang,' he thought. 'What shall I buy her? Some flowers, of course – and a little present. I'll take her a present each day.'

He knew how he was going to buy the flowers and the presents! He hadn't bothered to think it out for himself, or argue with his conscience – he just *knew* he was going to use the money that the gang had shared out with him the night before. Each boy had 74p, except Tom and Patrick, who had more because they had been the ones to get the money.

Bob slipped away from school in the dinner-hour and went to the flower shop. He bought a bunch of brilliant anemones. Then he went to the toy shop and bought a tiny doll in a cot. If he was careful, his money would last all the time Pat was in hospital.

The little girl was delighted to see him. She was sitting up against big pillows, looking rather pale. Her brown eyes were very large indeed, and she had a bright red ribbon in her hair. Bob thought she looked more like a pixie than ever.

She gave him a hug and smiled in delight at the flowers and the little doll. 'Oh, you *are* kind and generous!' she said. 'I knew you'd come and bring me a present. I just knew it. You're the nicest brother in the world!'

'Well, I couldn't let my little sister be ill and not bring her something, could I?' said Bob. 'Shall I read to you?'

'Yes. Mummy's coming soon and she'll talk to me,' said Pat. 'And Donald and Jeanie came in the dinner-hour, so that was fine. I like seeing people. It's lonely here all by myself – but the nurses are very nice to me. Will you come tomorrow, Bob?'

'Tomorrow and every day,' said Bob. 'Cheer up! You'll have a fine time here – and we'll give you an ENORMOUS welcome when you get home!'

By the end of the ten days all the money Bob had was spent on Pat. He didn't feel guilty. He didn't even think that he had done wrong. He thought of it as money for Pat, not for himself.

All the gang spent their money in different ways. When it was gone the same thought crept into all their minds – where was the next lot coming from?

CHAPTER SIXTEEN

## Christmas is Coming

Christmas was coming. Pat was home again. She was lively and happy once more, and would be going back to school after Christmas. She talked and talked about Bob.

'Bob said this and Bob said that. Bob gave me this and Bob is going to give me that!'

'Be quiet about Bob,' groaned Donald. '*We* gave you things too! There wasn't anything special about Bob's things!'

'There was,' said Pat. 'He knows *exactly* what I like! And he's going to give me a big doll for Christmas that shuts its eyes. So there!'

'Don't hope too much for that,' said Mrs Mackenzie, at once. 'That kind of doll is very expensive. I don't think Bob realizes the price. Dear old Bob – he's been very good to you, Pat.'

Mrs Mackenzie was grateful to Bob for coming in to play so often with Pat, now she was at home, and not going to school. She had him to tea each day, sad to know that the house next door was shut and locked till half-past six. The boy was intensely grateful for her cheerfulness and kindness. He did as much as he could for her without making Donald jealous.

'It's like having another son in the house,' she told her husband one night. 'He's so quick, too – sees at once when a thing wants doing and does it. He's a good boy, that, Andy. Don't you think so?'

'I do,' said Andy. 'He's a loyal boy too – never says a word against that selfish mother of his! Going out prettifying herself each day, neglecting the boy, and leaving him to himself as she does. I'd like to tell her what I think of her.'

'And I'd like to tell Mrs Berkeley what I think of *her*,' said Mrs Mackenzie. 'She's always in here complaining about Tom. He goes off each night and doesn't come back till all hours. She hasn't a notion where he goes to, she says. She's sure he's in bad company. But he never tells her a thing.'

'It's a pity Berkeley doesn't come back,' said her

husband. 'He's a weak fellow, it's true – but you can't afford to be weak when you've got children! You've got to find strength somewhere, or you'll let them down.'

'I'd like to knock their heads together,' said Mrs Mackenzie, digging her needles into her sewing as if she was digging it into Mrs Berkeley. 'Thinking of themselves all the time, while their boy is running wild, and their girls are perfect little miseries, as big whiners as their mother.'

They began to talk about Christmas. They would have the Christmas tree as usual, and the children could help to put up the decorations – they must really buy some more. And the Christmas puddings needed another boiling, and Aunt Katie had promised a fine turkey from her farm. What about the children's presents?

So they talked and planned for their family. Next door, at Summerhayes and at Hawthorns, things were quite different. There was plenty of talking and complaining at Summerhayes, but no planning! And there was neither talk *nor* planning at Hawthorns.

Bob's mother wanted to go away to her friend for Christmas. But she didn't want to take Bob. Bob would be in the way, because her friend's flat was very small. Also Bob was horrid these days – quite changed. His mother really disliked him, and wondered how she could get rid of him at Christmas-time.

'I couldn't bear to have Christmas here alone, with Bob sitting gloomy and sulky and rude opposite me,' she thought. 'I wonder if he'd like to go to his aunt's?'

She spoke to Bob about it. He looked at her in surprise. 'Go to Aunt Sue's for *Christmas*?' he said. 'Not have it at home? Will you be going too, then?'

'No, I've been asked somewhere else,' said his mother. 'But they can't have you. So I thought it would be lovely for you to go to Aunt Sue's, and be with her boys.'

'You know I don't like Aunt Sue and her namby-pamby little boys,' said Bob, furiously. 'You're getting rid of me, that's all.'

'I'm not,' said Mrs Kent, untruthfully. 'But you're so rude and horrid now, Bob. Honestly I think Christmas wouldn't be any fun here together.'

Bob glowered into the fire. He had rather looked forward to Christmas at Hawthorns. It was a nice little cottage, and he would have liked to decorate it. He meant to get a little tiny tree for Pat's bedroom and decorate that too. He had hoped that his mother might be nice to him at Christmas – but it was silly to hope anything!

'All right,' he said at last. 'You go where you want to go. I'll go to Aunt Sue's.'

He didn't mean to go to Aunt Sue's, though. He meant to sneak down into the cosy cellar belonging to the gang and have his Christmas Day there! Maybe the gang would come along in the evening and they could have some kind of feast and celebration. Bob began to plan it. Yes – it might be fun.

But again the question of money came up. You couldn't do anything without money. If only he was old enough to earn some money, how different things would be. But if you only had 5p a week, and no uncles or aunts came to visit you or give you a present of a 50p or 10p, you just couldn't buy anything!

And he had promised to get Pat a doll that opened and shut its eyes at Christmas-time. He counted up the days till Christmas. There weren't many!

He went down to the cellar that evening, and found the others there already. The place looked cosy, and Len had brought some paper-chains he had made at school, and put them up.

Bob looked round, pleased. He hadn't thought of

decorating their hidey-hole, but it would be a very good idea. He would bring some of the old decorations from home – they wouldn't be needed there this year – and he would make the place really gay.

'Those paper-chains look nice,' he told the delighted Len. 'We'll decorate this place. *I'll* do it. I've got plenty of red and green stuff and paper bells and things at home. I can make it look lovely. And I'll bring some holly too, out of our garden.'

'Your mother told my mother that you were going to your aunt's soon,' said Tom.

'Well, I'm not,' said Bob. 'I don't like her. My mother *thinks* I'm going – but I'm really coming down here! You must all come and join me in the evening and we'll have a party. I'll bring some food.'

'Good!' said Fred. 'A party for the gang. Anyone got any money tonight?'

Jack produced some. 'Where did you get it?' asked Fred.

'Ask no questions and you won't get no lies,' said Jack, grinning. The money was shared out. There was 42p each, with an extra 50p for Jack.

Bob wondered how much a doll would be that shut its eyes. More than 42p! How else could he get some money? Could he earn it?

But before he had tried to earn any the gang had plenty more! It was the next night, and five of them were down in the cellar. It was rather warm, and some of the boys had taken off their coats. Only Tom was missing. He hadn't been waiting outside the gate as usual for Bob to join him. Bob had been in to see Pat, and Mr Mackenzie had kept him talking.

Tom had gone off on his own. The others waited for him before beginning on some wood that Bob had brought.

They heard the low cautious whistle at last. Fred replied. The footsteps came down into the cellar. Tom's legs appeared – then his coat-hem – and finally Tom himself. He looked excited.

'Look here!' he said, kneeling down on the floor beside the low table. 'See what I found?'

He placed a wallet on the table. The others crowded round, breathing down each other's neck.

'A wallet!' said Fred, and took it up. 'Anything in it?'

'Look and see,' said Tom, jubilantly. Fred slid his fingers inside and pulled out a packet of £1 notes, all new and clean from the bank!

'Coo!' said Jack. 'Where did you get it?'

'I found it,' said Tom. 'On the pavement as I came here. I kicked against it – what do you think of that? Some luck, isn't it!'

'I should say it is!' said Patrick, his fingers itching to count the notes. 'Whose is it?'

'No name inside at all,' said Tom. 'There is a notebook with some notes scribbled in – and a bill for something or other – and a photograph of some girl – and the notes! That's all.'

'Well, finding's keeping,' said Fred, his eyes gleaming. 'And what a find! Let's count and see how much there is.'

There was thirty pounds in all. It was incredible. Thirty pounds – why, it was a small fortune! Len fingered the crisp notes with awe. He had never seen so much money in his life.

'I guess the fellow who lost it will be kicking himself!' said Jack. 'Come on – let's share it out. It will come in useful for Christmas! I might give my kid sisters something!'

They shared out. Five pounds each – what a lot of money. 'Good thing we don't know who lost the

money,' said Fred, pocketing his. 'We might feel we'd
got to give it back! Still, finding is keeping.'

Bob and Tom knew it wasn't, but they pretended
to themselves that it was. Tom knew what he was
going to buy – a new railway set! His mother had
sold his old one and now he would get a new one.

Bob knew what *he* was going to buy – a doll for
Pat, flowers for Mrs Mackenzie and books for Jeanie
and Donald. They deserved it, and they had been so
kind to him. He would spend every single penny of
the money on them.

But nothing on his mother. Nothing at all. Last
Christmas if he had had five pounds he would have
spent every bit of it on his mother. But things were
different now, thought Bob. She didn't love him, he
was a nuisance, she wanted to be rid of him. All right
– she shouldn't even have a cheap bunch of violets!

Bob had a wonderful spend in the next few days.
He ordered a plant for Mrs Mackenzie, a cyclamen
with lovely deep red flowers. He bought books for
Jeanie and Donald. He bought a pipe-scraper for Mr
Mackenzie, a ball for Frisky – and all the rest of the
money went on Pat!

He bought a big doll that shut its eyes whenever
it was laid down. How Pat would love that! Bob hid
the doll in his room – he didn't want his mother asking
awkward questions about how he had got the money
for it.

Then he hunted out all the old decorations they had
had for Christmas last year. He would make that cellar-
room look fine. Even if he had to spend all Christmas
Day there himself he'd have something gay to look
at, something cheerful. He guessed he'd have a better
time than Tom, anyway!

110

## CHAPTER SEVENTEEN

# Christmas-time

The day before Christmas came at last. There was great excitement at Barlings Cottage. The Christmas tree had come and was being decorated by the three children. Parcels were arriving by every post. Cards stood all along the mantelpiece and on the bookcases.

Frisky was as mad as the children. He tore here and there, barking when the postman came, barking when the tree fell over, barking at every single opportunity he had!

'I wish I could bark like that,' said Donald, standing perilously on the top of the ladder to pin up some holly-berry strands. '*I* should be barking all day long too! Isn't Christmas fun? I wonder how Bob and Tom are getting on. Mother, isn't it a shame, Bob's mother is going away for Christmas, and he's got to go to an aunt he doesn't like.'

'Oh dear – why didn't you tell me before? We could have had him here!' said Mrs Mackenzie. 'Poor boy. Mind you don't fall, Donald. Good gracious, do stop barking, Frisky. What is it now? The postman again?'

'I wish we could have Bob here,' said Pat. 'Mother, what's in that enormous box he brought me? It looks as if it might be a doll. Does it shut its eyes?'

'Now what *is* the good of asking me about any of your parcels before Christmas Day?' said her mother. 'Have I ever given away a Christmas secret yet? Don't waste your breath, Pat!'

'I bet it's a doll,' said Jeanie. 'He promised her one. He's left me something as well, hasn't he, Mother?'

'Yes, and something for Donald and Frisky and your father too,' said Mrs Mackenzie. 'He's a generous, warm-hearted boy. I'd like to have had him for Christmas. As for the plant he gave me, it's beautiful!'

'Yes. That couldn't be hidden because it had to be watered,' said Jeanie, looking at the cyclamen. 'I wonder if the Berkeleys are having as nice a time as we are. I saw the postman going there today.'

'Well, I hope their father sends them some nice things,' said Mrs Mackenzie. Everyone knew now that Mr Berkeley had gone away for good. The Mackenzie children had been horrified. They simply couldn't imagine what they would feel like if their own father went away.

'Mr Berkeley might come back for Christmas,' said Jeanie, hopefully. 'Hilda's hoping he will, but Eleanor says he won't. Mrs Berkeley isn't going to make a very nice Christmas for them, Eleanor says. She keeps crying all the time.'

Mrs Mackenzie could have said a lot of things about Mrs Berkeley and her behaviour but she didn't. She guessed things would be pretty miserable next door at Summerhayes this Christmas – and Hawthorns would be empty.

She was right about Summerhayes. Mrs Berkeley had told the three children that she didn't feel like Christmas, and had made very few preparations for it indeed. She had even said they wouldn't have any decorations because it seemed 'such a farce'.

'It may be a farce to her but it wouldn't be to us,' complained Hilda. 'This is going to be an awful Christmas – even worse than the last one when we first heard that Dad had lost his job.'

'Tom's such a beast nowadays too,' said Eleanor.

'Goes off every night almost and doesn't come back for ages. Do *you* know where he goes, Hilda?'

'No. I haven't any idea at all,' said Hilda. 'I don't care either. He's better out of the house with his rude, surly ways! I can't think why Mother keeps worrying about where he goes to. He can look after himself all right!'

Mrs Berkeley did worry about Tom and where he went, but she didn't take any real steps to find out. If he got into bad company, it was his father's fault, not hers, she thought. How could she manage a surly, rude boy like that on her own?

Mrs Kent departed to stay with her friend on the morning of the day before Christmas. She gave Bob £5 for his ticket to his aunt's and to buy a present for her and the boys. 'Catch the twelve o'clock train,' she said. 'Make yourself tidy. I've packed your bag for you. Have a good time, Bob – and a happy Christmas! You'll find a nice present from me in your bag.'

'Thank you,' said Bob, politely. 'Happy Christmas!'

He did not see his mother off. She let herself out and shut the front door. For one moment she felt inclined to go back and say she would stay with Bob. Then she shook herself. How silly! He didn't deserve a moment's thought. She ran to catch her train.

Bob didn't catch his. He looked at the £5 and calculated what to do with the money. He would spend some on food – and on ginger-beer. He would buy a small present for each of the gang. He might even get a tiny tree and decorate it and put it on the table in the cellar. He could hang it with the presents.

This was rather an exciting thought. He pictured the surprise of the gang when they saw the tree and the presents. Len would be off his head with delight. His family had never had a tree – nor had Jack's.

He went out shopping. He spent the evening decorating a tiny tree, and hanging it with the presents he had bought. The gang were not going to meet that night. They all had other things to do.

So Bob was the only one to creep down into the cellar. He carried a good many things – the little tree with its decorations and parcels. Two or three packets of food. A bag of mince pies which he intended to warm up over the top of the oil stove. Six bottles of ginger-beer – and a book to read while he was all alone in the cellar on Christmas Day.

He lighted the candle and the oil-stove. At once the place seemed cheerful and homely. Bob looked with pleasure at the decorations on the walls. He and the others had put them there the night before. They really did look gay. Holly gleamed there with red berries, and paper chains and loops and garlands of red and green hung around the walls. Paper bells hung down from the roof, and silver balls glittered here and there. Bob was very pleased indeed with everything.

He sat down on a box and looked round. He suddenly remembered how every Christmas his father had told him the story of the Shepherds and the Angels, and of the little Jesus in the manger. Tomorrow was the birthday of that baby. People would be going to church. He had gone too with his father and mother. All that seemed a hundred years ago!

'I'd like it back,' said Bob, aloud, and he felt lonely for those far-off days, when his father clapped him on the shoulder and told him he was a fine big boy, and his mother smiled and looked after them both.

He shook himself. He was being what Patrick called 'a softy'. Patrick jeered at softies and cowards and 'soppy folk'.

'You got to be tough these days,' he was always

saying to the others. 'Like the guys on the pictures. One of these days I'm going to get me a gun! I'll be a tough guy all right then.'

Bob slept alone at Hawthorns that night. He didn't dare to put the lights on in case Mrs Mackenzie saw them and wondered who was there. They all thought he had gone away to his aunt's.

He awoke early and got himself some breakfast. He undid the case his mother had packed for him and unpacked the parcel there that she had left. In it was a box with a beautiful new clockwork engine and trucks for his set. Bob stared at them for a long time and then put them aside. He preferred his old ones. His father had given him those.

He stole out of the house and made his way to the familiar hidey-hole. No one was about at all. He was very cautious, because it was daylight and no one must see where he went. It would be a dreadful thing if the hiding-place was discovered and they were all turned out. All the six boys had made it the centre of their lives — a bright, warm, cheerful spot, with friendly company and laughter.

But as Bob sat peacefully down there that day, dreadful things were happening. He didn't know anything about them till the evening. He sat there, eating and drinking and reading his book, waiting patiently for the others to come when it was dark.

But they didn't come.

The dreadful happenings had all begun with Patrick. When the boy had gone home with the crisp new £1 notes in his pocket some nights before, his father had found them. He had taken one of them away from Patrick, and told him he could keep the others.

'Where you got them from I don't care to know,' said his father. 'But one of them I'm keeping for meself,

116

Patrick boy! You wouldn't grudge your old father one, would you now?'

Patrick *had* grudged his father the £1 note, but he didn't dare say so. He was only too glad to find he was allowed to keep four for himself. He spent them as soon as he could, fearful that they too might be taken away from him.

His father had spent the £1 note at a tobacconist's shop, buying himself cigarettes. The man looked at him sharply when he took the £1 note. He also looked at the number on the note.

'Will you wait for a moment while I get change?' he said, and went to the room at the back of the shop. He telephoned the police.

'Johnson, Tobacconist, Rowton Road here,' he said in a low voice, when the police answered. 'You know those new £1 notes that were reported lost to you the other day – and you were given the numbers by the bank? You told us to look out for any that might be passed on to us. Well, one's just come in. The man is here in my shop. Do you want to question him? I'll keep him talking till you come. Right.'

He went back to the shop and counted out the change very slowly. He knocked a coin on to the floor and took a very long time finding it, talking all the time.

Before he had picked it up, two policemen walked in. 'Where's the note, Mr Johnson?' asked one. The tobacconist silently passed it over. The policeman looked at the number and nodded. He turned to Patrick's father, who was looking surprised and fearful.

'You passed that note over the counter to Mr Johnson just now,' said the policeman. 'Where did you get it?'

'From my son!' blurted out the man. 'It's nothing

117

to do with me. He gave it to me himself. It was my son Patrick that brought it home.'

'We'll question him then,' said the policeman. 'He'll be taken to the police station and asked where he got it. Where is he?'

And twenty minutes later Patrick, who despised cowards and softies and those who split on their pals, told the whole story of Tom bringing in the wallet a few nights back – and he gave the names of the whole of the gang!

CHAPTER EIGHTEEN

## The Police!

That was on Christmas Eve. Later on, detectives went knocking at several doors.

They knocked on Jack's door, and his whole frightened family listened to the policemen's questions. Poor Jack was taken to the police station, with his mother and father beside him, and charged with receiving money he knew to have been stolen by finding.

'But finding's keeping,' said Jack, tears streaming down his face.

'Did your parents teach you that?' asked the policeman. 'More shame to them then. They know that's not right.'

The police went knocking at Fred's door too, and he and Len had to go to the police station to be charged, with their mother to accompany them, angry and loud-voiced, but frightened.

And the police went to the Berkeleys' house too. For one wild moment when the knock sounded at the door the three children thought it was their father come back again. Eleanor rushed to the door. She opened it and found herself staring at two tall policemen.

'Is your father in, missy?' asked one. 'Or your mother?'

'Mother is, but my father's away,' said Eleanor. The policemen stepped inside. 'I'll tell Mother you want to speak to her,' gasped Eleanor, and fled.

Tom came out into the hall. When he saw the police he stopped, and his heart went cold. He was about to go back into the room when one of the policemen spoke to him.

'Is your name Tom Berkeley?'

Before he could answer Mrs Berkeley came out, looking white. 'Oh what is it?' she said. 'Has anything happened to my husband?'

'We haven't come about your husband,' said one policeman. 'I'm afraid we've come about this boy here. We'll have to ask him some questions, and he may have to go to the police station with us and be charged with an offence.'

Mrs Berkeley gave a scream and sat down on a hall-chair. 'Tom! Tom! What have you done?'

'Nothing,' said Tom, white-faced. 'I don't know what they mean.'

'You belong to a gang, I believe,' said the first policeman, opening his notebook. 'The Six Terrors Gang. The others are the following' – and he gave their names. 'Is that so?'

'Yes. I do belong,' said Tom, full of anxiety. How did the police know about the gang? They had all sworn not to split.

'We have questioned the boys Patrick, Leonard, Frederick and Jack,' said the policemen, referring to his notebook. 'We are inquiring into a matter of a wallet containing new £1 notes, numbers of which were given

119

to us when the loss was reported. The other boys all say that you brought this wallet to the gang – and that the money was shared out between you. Is that right?'

'No, no, no!' screamed Mrs Berkeley. 'You've made a mistake, constable. It can't be my son. He wouldn't do a thing like that. He'd take the wallet to the police station. He knows better than to steal.'

'The wallet was lost, and the other boys say that your son found it and brought it to them,' said the policeman, patiently. He turned to Tom.

'Is that correct?' he asked.

Tom collapsed. His knees began to shake. He gazed round for help, but there was none to be had. His mother was sobbing hysterically, his sisters were clinging together crying. Where was his father? His father would have stood by him and helped him!

Tom clung to a chair-back and looked dumbly at the policemen. They looked gravely back. 'Will you answer my question?' said one.

'Yes,' said Tom, in a whisper. 'I did find the wallet. We shared the money out.'

'Will you come to the police station with your son, ma'am?' asked the policeman. 'He must be charged there.'

'Oh no, no,' moaned Mrs Berkeley. 'Oh, I can't believe this is true. It isn't true, constable, it isn't. You'll find my son isn't guilty.'

'Maybe so, ma'am,' said the policeman stolidly. 'I hope so, for your sake. He'll certainly have a chance to tell us all about it when he comes before the Juvenile Court.'

Mrs Berkeley sobbed again. The Juvenile Court! Fancy Tom having to go there. Why, they might take him away and send him to some strict school where she wouldn't see him for a long long time!

'About this sixth boy,' said the other policeman. 'Robert Kent. I believe he lives just near by. We could take him to the station at the same time.'

'He's away,' said Eleanor, wiping her eyes. 'He's gone to stay with his aunt. His mother's away too, but I don't know where.'

'We'll have to leave him till he gets back then,' said the policeman. 'Are you ready, ma'am?'

So it was that Bob was the only one not visited by the police on Christmas Eve. He was at home of course, alone, and in the dark, but nobody guessed. Only Tom knew, and in his fear and anxiety he had forgotten that Bob would not be away at his aunt's.

The police soon knew everything. All the boys broke down and confessed what they knew. Poor frightened little Len even told about the money that had been taken from the cash-box belonging to the old newsagent not far from the cellar.

'Ah – so it was your gang that took that too, was it?' asked the policeman. 'Where did you all meet, by the way?'

And so the secret of the cellar hiding-place was told too. 'We'll go there tomorrow,' said the police. 'It won't run away! Now mind – not one of you boys is to go near that place again.'

The next day was Christmas Day, of course. Five scared, miserable boys woke up that morning, remembering the night before. Tom was the most miserable of the lot! He had spoilt Christmas for everyone.

Eleanor and Hilda treated him as if he was an outcast. They wouldn't go near him. His mother reproached him and poured scorn on him and wept.

'What your father will say I don't know,' she kept saying.

'I want him,' said Tom. 'Ask him to come as soon as he can. I don't care what he says to me, I just want him. He shouldn't have gone away. I wouldn't have done all the things I did if he'd been here – not such bad ones anyway.'

Only Bob was blissfully unaware of all these happenings. He was down in the cellar still, waiting for the others. He looked at the little Christmas tree when six o'clock came, and wondered if he should light the candles on it. It would be nice for the others to come down and see the tree shining brightly.

He listened for the gang. They were late. Why didn't they come? Perhaps they were all having rather a long-drawn-out Christmas tea. Except Patrick. He had no mother to get him tea.

Bob yawned. He was getting bored. And then he heard sounds above. Ah – that must be the gang coming!

He listened again. Yes – someone was moving about among the rubble and fallen bricks. He would light the Christmas tree candles!

He struck a match and lighted the candles. They were small, but they flamed up well. The little tree looked lovely.

Footsteps began to come down the steps. Bob listened for the gang whistle. It didn't come. An uneasy feeling crept over him. Whose footsteps were these? They sounded too heavy for any of the gang.

Two big feet appeared down the steps. Legs in dark-blue trousers. A policeman's cape – and finally the whole policeman stood there, helmet and all, a lamp in his hand.

Bob was so utterly amazed and terrified that he couldn't say a word, or make a movement. Another policeman arrived and stood beside the first. They stared in astonishment at the gaily-decorated cellar.

'Look at this,' said one. 'A home from home! All decorated up, and a tree with candles burning too. Carpets on the floor, and what's that – a telephone?'

'Toy one,' said the other. Then he noticed Bob for the first time. The boy had been in the shadows and had kept so still that neither of the policemen had seen him. But now that their eyes were used to the candlelight and shadows they saw him clearly.

'Hallo – there's a boy!' said one. 'Another of the gang, I suppose. I thought there were only six.'

Bob stared, speechless. Did they know about the gang then?

'What's your name, boy?' asked one of the policemen.

'Robert Kent,' whispered Bob.

'Ah – this *is* the sixth!' said the policeman. 'What's he doing here, though? We were told he had gone away to stay with his aunt. Stand up, boy. We've questions to ask you.'

Bob stood up on trembling legs. He was terribly frightened. Suddenly the jolly, cheerful, exciting gang he had belonged to appeared as something quite different – it was really what the police thought it to be, a company of bad little boys, ready to steal or do mean tricks for which they could be severely punished. All the make-believe went, and Bob saw the gang as it really was.

He answered the questions in a trembling voice. He told the truth. The police felt sorry for this lonely boy down in the cellar.

'Who did all this?' said one, pointing to the gay decorations. 'And who lighted the candles on the tree?'

'I did,' said Bob.

'What are these on the tree – these little parcels?' said the other man.

'Presents I got for the others,' said Bob. 'They're –

they're pretty miserable at home, sir, so I just got the tree and things for a treat.'

'Are you miserable at home too?' asked one of the men. Bob hesitated. He didn't want to say anything that might make the police think poorly of his mother.

'All right. You needn't answer that,' said the man. 'Look, we want you to come to the police station with us. Is there any grown-up who would come with you? Your mother's away, I understand.'

Bob stood looking at the men with anxious eyes. Would Mr Mackenzie go with him? He might. If only, only he would!

CHAPTER NINETEEN

## Two Scared Boys

The police went knocking at the Mackenzies' next, with Bob trembling between them. What a shock for that family!

Mrs Mackenzie went to the door, and Donald, Jeanie, Pat and Frisky crowded after her. Who was this on Christmas evening?

'Can I have a word in private with you, madam?' said one of the policemen. Looking startled, Mrs Mackenzie took the two men and Bob into the dining-room. The sitting-room door was closed on the three children. Mr Mackenzie joined the police too, looking grave.

Mrs Mackenzie put her arm round Bob. What *could* the boy have been doing? And why wasn't he with his aunt and her family?

The police told her and her husband the whole story

as shortly as possible. They listened in silence. Tears ran down Mrs Mackenzie's face as she heard the little cellar described, all decorated, and with a little Christmas tree lighted. She held Bob tightly. If only she'd known! He could have been with them!

'We know his mother is away, but Bob says he doesn't know her address,' said the policeman. 'He wondered if one of you would come along to the police station with him? He's got to be charged, and there must be someone with him, as he's a child.'

'We'll both come,' said Mr Mackenzie, with a glance at his wife. 'What you say may all be true, officer – but we can vouch for this boy ourselves. We're as fond of him as if he were our own son. He's a grand fellow, but he's been neglected – had no homelife at all lately! Can we take him back with us here tonight? He can't go and stay in that empty house alone – Christmas night and all.'

'That would be kind of you,' said the policeman. He patted Bob on the shoulder. 'I'm glad you've got good friends to speak for you,' he said. 'That makes a lot of difference. If somebody gives you a good character that will help you when you come before the court.'

Bob was in a daze. He scarcely knew what was happening. He went to the police station, hardly heard what was said, and went back to the Mackenzies' house again.

'He'd better go straight to bed, I think,' said Mrs Mackenzie. 'He's not fit for any jollification – and ours must have their bit of fun, in spite of all this. We'll just tell them Bob is in a bit of trouble and we're having him until his mother comes back. He can sleep in the little back room. I'll make up the bed. Come along, Bob. I'm going to put you to bed, and bring you a nice supper.'

Donald, Jeanie and Pat were alarmed and upset. What was happening? Their father went in to them and told them a little. Jeanie began to cry.

'Will he be sent to prison? Why did the police come?'

Pat burst into tears too. 'What's Bob done? Bob's good! I'll tell that big policeman Bob is good. He bought me that lovely doll, and he's my big brother. I won't let people hurt Bob.'

'You can go and say goodnight to him when he's in bed,' said Mrs Mackenzie, suddenly thinking it would be a good idea. Take Frisky too.'

And so when poor tired, dazed Bob was tucked in bed after a simple supper of bread and milk, the door opened and in came Pat. She ran to the bed, and Bob felt two arms round his neck, almost strangling him. Then Frisky jumped up on the bed and began to lick his face vigorously.

'I don't care what you've done, Bob,' said Pat. 'And I don't believe you'd ever do wrong! Anyway I don't care. I love you!'

'Wuff,' said Frisky, meaning exactly the same thing. He pawed at Bob, and Bob hugged both Pat and Frisky together, feeling happier.

Mrs Mackenzie called Pat after a minute or two, and the little girl gave Bob another hug and went. But Frisky stayed behind. He cuddled up in bed beside the boy, and Bob was very glad. He put his hand down by Frisky, and Frisky gave it a lick every now and again till the boy was asleep.

Mrs Mackenzie kept Bob with her till his mother came back three days later. She and Mr Mackenzie had a long talk with him. He told them everything, not keeping back one single detail.

'You know that Tom is in trouble over this too?' said Mr Mackenzie. 'I hear that his father has come

126

back today. His mother sent him a telegram, and he has come back to stand by Tom.'

'I'm glad,' said Bob. 'I wish *I* had a father to stand by me. I know my mother won't. She'll be so angry when she knows I've taken cushions and carpets and an oil stove for our cellar room. She thinks I'm a nuisance now, you know. Nobody really wants me; I knew that, so it just seemed as if it didn't matter *what* I did!'

'Yes. That's quite understandable but very wrong, Bob,' said Mr Mackenzie. 'It *always* matters what we do, no matter whether we feel unhappy or don't-carish or savage because the world seems to use us badly. You see, what we do affects other people as well as ourselves. For instance, Pat is very unhappy over this – and I'm sure you didn't want to hurt Pat.'

'No, I didn't,' said Bob, wretchedly. 'I love Pat. If I'd

ever had a sister I'd have wanted one like Pat. I'm terribly, terribly sorry now for everything, I can't think how I came to do it all, I really can't. Sharing in all that money when I knew it was someone else's! But I never spent a penny of it on myself, Mr Mackenzie. I spent it all on Pat when she was in hospital − and on all of you for Christmas.'

The Mackenzies looked at one another. They believed Bob. They were sure he hadn't spent one penny on himself, they were sure he was sorry. They were also certain that he would never do such a thing again − if he had the chance of being loved, and felt that he was wanted by somebody.

'I'll never in my life behave like this again,' said Bob. 'I know I wouldn't have if my father had been alive. I wouldn't have done it either if my mother hadn't gone out to work. Things got different then somehow. I know lots of other mothers go out to work and aren't home, like you are, to welcome their children and get them their tea − but I bet all those kids hate it as much as I did! I did hate coming home to that cold, dark empty house. I never, never want to go there again.'

There were long talks going on at Tom's house too. Mr Berkeley had come back immediately he had got the frantic telegram. 'Tom in serious trouble,' the telegram had said. 'Come back at once.'

He had cut short his wife's complaints and reproaches and tears.

'I want to hear what Tom has to say,' he said. 'I'll go to the police too and hear their story − but I want Tom's first. Tell me the truth, Tom.'

Tom told him the truth. Tom was sullen and bitter and defiant now. He stood facing his parents and his sisters, and spared them no detail of his misdoings. His mother sobbed as she heard what he had done each evening when he had gone out for hours. His father groaned when he heard about the wallet Tom had found and kept.

'You know perfectly well you should have taken it to the police station,' he said. 'You know that finding isn't keeping. How could you do these things!'

'Don't blame *me*,' said Tom, resentfully. 'You and Mother can take the blame! What sort of a home do you think this has ever been for me – or for the girls? Nagging and bickering and rowing in front of us ever since we can remember! No peace, no pulling together like the Mackenzies. I've hated my home for a long time, and so have you, Dad, or you wouldn't have cleared out. I just did what you did – cleared out too, every evening.'

There was a silence, only broken by Mrs Berkeley's crying, but nobody took any notice of that.

'I blame myself bitterly for leaving you all now,' said Mr Berkeley, at last. 'This might not have happened if I'd been here to see to you, Tom.'

Tom looked at him. 'Oh yes, it would have happened!' he said. 'It was beginning to happen before you went. Don't you remember the cinema affair? I'm a bad lot! And I don't care! I don't care even if I have to go to prison. It'll serve you all right for making things so beastly at home!'

'Tom, Tom,' said his father, covering his face with his hand. 'Don't say things like that. I was always proud of you in so many ways. What have we done to you, Tom?'

Tom's mouth began to tremble. He pursed it defiantly. Ah, Tom was being a 'tough guy' – he wasn't going to give in, or say he was sorry. He had been terribly frightened at first, but his mother had reproached him, and the girls had been so disgusted and ashamed that he had worked himself up into a rage. All right — if he was so bad, so mean, so much of a villain, he'd *be* one!

Not even his father could do much with the defiant boy. He gave it up after a time. Perhaps Tom would think differently in a day or two.

He spoke seriously to his wife. 'I'm coming back again, my dear, to see if we can do better. I'm going to play my part and you must play yours. We *must* give Tom a home he wants to stay in — and the girls too. They will be off and away as soon as they can leave if we don't give them the security and kindness they want. No, don't say anything, and stop crying. We haven't got to think of ourselves now. This is serious for Tom, you realize that, don't you?'

His wife dried her eyes. 'I still think it's more your fault than mine,' she said. 'But some of it is my fault, I see that now. I'll try again, but it's dreadful to have Tom in disgrace like this! The girls are so ashamed — and what will everyone say?'

'Shall I tell you what people will say?' said Mr Berkeley. 'They will say, "It's the parents' fault! They didn't make a happy home for those children!" That's what they will say, my dear! It's our shame, as much as Tom's!'

Those were miserable days for everyone concerned in the matter — but perhaps the least unhappy of the six boys was Bob. He was the only one who was sincerely sorry, sincerely shocked with himself, and meant to turn over a new leaf.

## CHAPTER TWENTY

## The Law Gets to Work

Bob's mother took the whole affair in a most extraordinary way. Mrs Mackenzie was watching for her to come back, and when she saw her going in to the house next door she went in to see her.

With a grave face she told Mrs Kent what had happened to Bob. She told her how Bob had not gone to his aunt's but had prepared a Christmas feast and celebration down in the cellar room – and how the police had found him there. She could not resist adding a few reproachful words.

'How you, his mother, could have gone off to a friend's, when you must have known it would make the boy unhappy, I cannot imagine,' she said. 'Surely a mother's place is with her children at Christmas-time?'

Mrs Kent stared at her coldly. 'It's no business of yours what I do,' she said. 'You're pleased my Bob has got into trouble, aren't you? Your children are all perfect, aren't they? You're *the* perfect mother, aren't you? Oh, I know what people like you are like – going round preaching at others, and gloating when they go wrong.'

'Don't say things like that,' said Mrs Mackenzie, really distressed. 'You know they aren't true. Why, I've had Bob with us ever since the police brought him, and I've mothered him and been as kind as I could. We love the boy – he's a fine youngster. I should have thought you would have been glad to know someone was looking after Bob for you, and . . .'

'You can keep him, for all I care,' said Mrs Kent. 'I don't want him back here. You tell me he took things from his home to furnish this cellar-place, wherever it is. Stealing from his own mother! It's wicked! He's a really bad boy. I'm ashamed to think he's my son!'

Mrs Mackenzie looked in disgust at Bob's mother. 'Listen, Mrs Kent,' she said. 'I can see into your real thoughts. You know this is all your fault, don't you – leaving Bob so much by himself – and you feel guilty, but you're not going to admit it! So you're putting up a show of anger and disgust with Bob. But you feel guilty in your inmost mind, don't you?'

Mrs Mackenzie was so exactly right that for a moment Mrs Kent was taken aback. But she was an obstinate woman and was not going to admit anything of the sort. She *did* feel guilty about Bob, she knew she had been selfish and neglectful, but she was not going to admit it to anyone! Let Bob bear the blame for everything, the wicked boy!

'I can see it's no use trying to make you stand by Bob,' said Mrs Mackenzie at last. 'But what he will feel like when I have to tell him what you've said, and that you won't let him come home, I can't imagine. Will you please let the police know you're back? They want to see you.'

For the first time Mrs Kent looked alarmed. 'Do *I* have to see the police?' she said.

'Of course. You're Bob's mother,' said Mrs Mackenzie. 'And in any case when the boys are brought before the police court you will have to be there. All the parents have to be there, so that the magistrate may find out exactly how much the fathers and mothers are to blame for their children's wrong-doing.'

She left without another word. Poor Bob! How

difficult to tell him that his mother wasn't going to stand by him.

But Bob was not as upset as she had expected him to be. 'I knew she wouldn't,' he said. 'I think she'll be glad to be rid of me, really. I do want her very badly, but not if she doesn't want *me*. I suppose I'll be sent away somewhere, won't I, Mrs Mackenzie? I shall miss you all dreadfully. Shall I be sent away to some strict school somewhere?'

Mrs Mackenzie didn't know. She was worried. Oh, what a pity she hadn't known that Bob had not gone to his aunt's that Christmas! But even then she couldn't have stopped these things from happening.

A date was fixed for the six boys to attend the Juvenile Court in the district, and for their parents to attend too. Len and Fred were frightened, and Jack was very upset. Patrick was defiant. What did *he* care! He'd do it all again if he could. But secretly he was afraid too. What exactly would the magistrate do to him?

Tom was also defiant, but mostly because he could see that it was hurting his parents, and he was trying to punish them for having made him miserable. He *was* sorry now for his share in the escapades, but he wasn't going to say so. No, he was going to strut and be a 'tough guy' and defy everyone.

'If you behave like that at the Court you will be foolish, Tom,' said his father.

The machinery of the law was now working in this Case of the Six Boys. Headmasters of their various schools were being asked to report on the boys' behaviour and work at school. A woman Probation Officer of the Court visited each boy's home to find out the home conditions, and what the parents had to say.

She saw Jack's crowded home. She was shouted at by Patrick's father, who told her he had beaten Patrick every single day. He, also, was being charged for taking one of the £1 notes from Pat, knowing that it had been stolen.

She went to Len's and Fred's home, and saw their dirty, don't care mother. She went to Tom's house and sat quite still and silent while she listened to Mrs Berkeley saying bad things about her husband, and Mr Berkeley admitting that he had left his home and children.

She then went to Hawthorns and saw Mrs Kent, young, pretty, but hard-faced and full of tales against Bob. She had even dug up some small misdeeds from his back years to try and make the officer think that Bob had always been bad.

'You go out to work, I believe?' said the Probation Officer smoothly, making notes. 'And let me see – what time do you get back?'

'Half-past six,' said Mrs Kent. 'But don't you begin to think that's anything to do with Bob's going wrong. He's always been a difficult boy, always. Especially since his father died. He won't come back here, he says. Some friends have got him now.'

'What is their name and address?' asked the officer at once. Mrs Kent gave it, wishing she hadn't said anything about Bob's not being with her. Now that preachy Mrs Mackenzie would go and say good things about that bad boy!

She did, of course. The officer asked her a great many questions and she answered them truthfully. Mr Mackenzie came in half-way through and he said a good deal too.

'The boy's a good boy. He's sorry and ashamed, and this has been such a lesson to him that I'm certain he'll never do such a thing again,' said Mr Mackenzie. 'I'd trust him as I trust my own son Donald!'

'Thank you. You've been very helpful,' said the woman officer, getting up. 'Bob's a lucky boy to have such good friends.'

A great many people were due to appear at the Juvenile Court in the case of the six boys. Not only the boys and their parents, but also the old newsagent whose money had been stolen, a woman who had seen Patrick and Tom running away, the man whose wallet had been found, and even the cinema manager who had once caught Tom and Bob in his cinema. Len and Fred and Jack confessed to many misdeeds, and there were people appearing concerned with those too.

The day came. The six boys all remembered it when they awoke, and not one of them wanted to get up! What would their punishment be? What was the Court like? Would the magistrate be very stern?

The boys had all been told that they were much too young to be sent to prison, but Len was still afraid he might be. His mother kept saying he would be, and this frightened him very much.

Jeanie, Donald and Pat knew that it was the day for Bob to go to Court. Frisky seemed to know too. He kept jumping up at Bob and licking him whenever he could.

Bob had been feeling much happier since he had been with the Mackenzies. Life was so serene there. There was no bad feeling, no spite, no nagging. They all made him very welcome, and Pat was so lively and talkative that her mother was astonished.

'It's because she's got someone to notice her and play with her, I suppose,' she thought. 'Bob is really very good with her. She's quite forgotten to mourn about being one-on-her-own!'

The Juvenile Court was held in a small hall at the

other end of the town. At the time stated everyone was there, sitting in a room outside the hall itself. The six boys grinned sheepishly at each other and then looked away.

They all wondered what had happened to their hideout, the cellar. The police had dismantled it, and now it was empty, damp and cold. Most of the things had gone back to their owners, the greatest number to Bob's mother, who had recognized dozens of articles.

All the parents were there. Mr and Mrs Mackenzie had brought Bob, of course, and had then left. His mother was there, sitting a little way away, her face white and grim. She didn't like sitting near Jack's mother, or Len's: such dirty, disgusting women, she thought! Surely their boys weren't the ones that Bob had gone with — how terrible!

And now the names of the six boys were being called in a loud voice.

'Thomas Berkeley! Robert Kent! Patrick O'Shea! Jack Harris! Frederick Ross! Leonard Ross! Come this way, please. The parents also.'

### CHAPTER TWENTY-ONE

## *At the Juvenile Court*

With a clattering of feet the six boys followed the usher into the Court. Their parents followed. Everyone felt solemn and nervous. There was a table at one end of the Court, with a high window behind. The light fell straight on to the scared faces of the six boys. Three people sat at the table, two men and a woman, children's magistrates.

At the back of the Court sat a police inspector in uniform. Other men and women sat here and there round the Court, some busy with papers. The two policemen who had gone knocking at the doors were there also, in uniform.

There was a silence as the chief magistrate glanced through some papers. Then he looked sternly at the boys, and finally he addressed Tom.

'You, Thomas Berkeley, have been brought here because the police say that you stole by finding a wallet containing £30 in notes. Did you do that?'

'Yes, sir,' said Tom.

The magistrate turned to the other five boys. 'And you five boys are said to have received some of this money, well knowing it to have been stolen. Now is that correct?'

'Yes, sir,' they each answered, in turn.

The magistrate then asked the policeman to tell the Court the facts of the case. The six boys looked at him, scared, as he stepped into the witness-box and related all that had happened.

He also described how Bob had been found down in the cellar on Christmas Day.

'He dressed a little Christmas tree, and hung it with presents for the rest of the gang,' said the policeman, amid a dead silence. The gang looked round at Bob. This was the first they knew of the Christmas tree! Good old Bob! How all wished they had seen the tree. Bob hung his head. That Christmas night seemed a long time ago now, but he could suddenly see the gaily-decorated cellar, and that little tree lit with candles.

The magistrate listened closely. When the policeman had finished his story he stepped from the witness-box, and the magistrate looked sternly at all the six boys.

'All this is very serious,' he said, and the boys looked

137

at him fearfully. 'Very wrong indeed. I want to hear
what you have each got to say about it. Thomas, didn't
you know it was wrong to keep that money?'

'Yes, sir,' said Tom, going scarlet.

'Robert Kent – did *you* know it was wrong?'

'Yes, sir, and I'm sorry,' said Bob, in a low voice.

'Patrick O'Shea, what do *you* say about it?' asked
the magistrate.

'No, sir, I didn't think it was wrong,' said Patrick
at once. 'It was found, sir. And finding's keeping,
everyone knows that.'

'Finding is *not* keeping,' said the magistrate, sternly.
'You know that as well as I do, Patrick. Come nearer
to me. Now listen; if I gave you a £10 note and you
went out and lost it, and somebody found it and kept
it, without trying to find out whose it was, so that
you didn't get it back, wouldn't you think it was wrong
of the boy?'

'Yes, sir,' said Patrick at once.

'And what would you do to the boy if he were caught?' asked the magistrate.

'I'd want to see him punished. I'd bang him on the head, sir,' said Patrick, fiercely.

'I'm glad you see what I'm getting at,' said the magistrate, dryly. 'Stand back. Jack Harris, did *you* think that finding was keeping?'

'Yes, sir,' said Jack.

A cry came from behind him. It was Jack's mother. 'Oh, he didn't think so, sir. I've taught him different. Jack knew it was wrong.'

'Yes. I am sure he did,' said the magistrate. 'You Frederick, and you Leonard – you're brothers, aren't you? What have you to say about it?'

Len began to cry bitterly. Fred looked at the magistrate miserably. 'Yes, sir – I guess we knew it was wrong,' he said.

'Anything known about these boys?' asked the magistrate.

A man stepped forward. He had a sheaf of papers in his hand. He told the magistrates a little about the homes of each of the children, and everyone listened intently. Homes were so important!

'I have the boys' school reports here, sir,' said the man, and he placed a copy of each report before the magistrates. The boys looked at one another nervously. What had their Headmasters said about them? How they all wished they had behaved well at school, and could get a good report! You just never knew when a fine report would be important.

'Thomas Berkeley. Your Head says you have good brains and can work well. He also says you are moody and not co-operative, and resentful of discipline. He also reports that you were one of the boys who broke into the cinema one night and attended a show without paying.' The magistrate looked up at Tom.

Tom said nothing, but looked defiant. All right — let everyone blame him!

'Are his parents here?' asked the magistrate. 'Ah — will you come right up, please? What have you to say about this boy? Is he good at home? Obedient? Helpful? Can you tell me why he has got into bad company and bad ways? He apparently comes from a decent home.'

'He's a difficult boy and a surly one,' began his mother. 'He's made us all ashamed of him. His father can't manage him, and nor can anyone. You see . . .'

'Wait a moment,' said the magistrate. 'I will hear this without the boys being here. They can go out for a minute — their parents too.'

The boys and the other parents clattered out. The door shut. The magistrate looked sternly at Mrs

Berkeley. 'I have a report here from the Probation Officer who called to see you,' he said. 'It is not a good report, Mrs Berkeley. It looks as if Thomas got into bad ways because you made the boy unhappy.'

'Oh, how wicked of that woman to say that!' cried Mrs Berkeley. Her husband put his hand on her arm and stopped her. He turned to the magistrate and spoke humbly.

'The report is correct, sir. The home was unhappy – it still is, for that matter. I cleared out and left. I shouldn't have done that. We – we don't get on well, sir, my wife and I. And that comes hard on the children. The boy's not really to blame, sir.'

The magistrate asked a few more questions. Then he asked for Tom to be brought back again, and told his parents to go out of the court. It was Tom's turn to be frank about his home!

The magistrate looked at the sullen boy. 'Your parents say that you have been unhappy at home, Thomas,' he said, 'and they say that it was not really your fault that you got into bad company. Were you unhappy at home?'

'Yes. Very,' said Tom. 'I hated it – all that nagging and bickering and crying, and taking sides. And if I go back home again it'll all begin again, sir, and I'll hate it again, and run off. I'm not sorry I did what I did – I had to. It was exciting – and – well, I felt I was paying everyone out for being beastly to me.'

'I see,' said the magistrate. 'But there are plenty of people who are unhappy and yet don't go wrong. You *look* as if you have a strong character, but it seems to me it must be very weak if you run away from things like that.'

' 'Tisn't weak,' said Tom. 'I could do all right if people backed me up. I hate my home!'

The magistrate said no more to Tom, but told the usher to bring the boy's parents back into the Court again. They came in. Mrs Berkeley was sobbing. Mr Berkeley stood pale and distressed. What a failure he and his wife had made of things!

The magistrate conferred with the others sitting at the table with him. Then he turned to Tom.

He spoke sternly but kindly. 'We are going to put you on probation for two years. We believe there is a lot of good in you, Thomas, but we think that you will do better away from home, at any rate for a little while. We are going to make a condition of your probation that you go right away to a school in the country, where we hope you will be happy and do well. You will have to be there for six months at least, and perhaps for a whole year.'

'Oh no, no!' cried Mrs Berkeley. 'Don't send him right away from us! His father will manage him now he's come back. Oh, the disgrace – don't, don't send Tom away!'

'He will be allowed to come home when his time is up, on two conditions,' said the magistrate, sternly. 'One is if he has learned his lesson and we get good reports of him from the Headmaster of the school where we shall send him – and the other condition is if we are satisfied that there is a good and happy home for him to come back to. It is not altogether his fault that this boy has gone wrong, and that is why we are not punishing him as severely as we might. You understand that you must play your part too?'

'Yes, sir,' said Mr Berkeley, and Mrs Berkeley dabbed her eyes and nodded. The magistrate turned to Tom.

'You must repay to your Probation Officer out of your own pocket-money £5, which is your share of the £30,' he said to the boy. 'Now Tom – good luck to you! Show us that you've got a strong character and not a weak one, after all!'

'Yes, sir,' said Tom, still sulky – but he was very scared at the idea of being sent away to an 'approved' school in the country. He would be very lonely and cut off from everyone.

Then Bob was dealt with. The magistrate was gentler on him. He had the reports about Bob's mother before him – and many a time before he had had similar reports of children going wrong because their mothers had left them in order to go out to work.

Bob's mother was there, hard-faced and determined not to be blamed. The magistrate questioned Bob and could get very little out of him. He didn't want to speak against his mother. The magistrate called Mrs Kent forward.

'I see that you leave the house before this boy goes to school and don't return till half-past six, and you lock the door so that he can't get in,' said the magistrate. 'What about his tea?'

'He's got friends who'll give it to him,' said Mrs Kent. 'I *have* to leave the door locked. He'd smash the place up if I didn't. Why, once he . . .'

'I don't think we want to hear that,' said the magistrate. 'I see that you have said you don't want the boy back home? You complain that he is completely out of control – rude, disobedient, and destructive – also that he has stolen many articles from you for his cellar home. He is your only child. Don't you think you could give up your work and care for him again?'

'No,' said Mrs Kent. 'I'm ashamed of him. He'll only get worse. I want to sell up and go right away out of the district, I feel so ashamed. And I don't want him to come with me. He's a bad boy.'

The magistrate again conferred with the others at the table. He spoke kindly to Bob.

'You hear what your mother says? What do you think about it?'

Bob didn't look at his mother. 'I don't want to stand in her way, sir,' he said. 'I'd be in her way now, I know. She doesn't want me. But oh, sir – what's going to happen to me? Have I got to go to that school too?'

'No, Robert,' said the magistrate. 'We have good reports of you as well as bad ones – and the good ones are so good that we are going to give you a chance. We feel that you are not having enough home-life, and the Probation Officer has found some very nice people who have offered to provide a home for you, and to be foster-parents to you.'

'Where will it be?' said Bob, in dread. 'Far away? Away from my school – and – and my friends?'

'I'm afraid so,' said the magistrate.

Poor Bob! No mother, no home, no friends. He went out of the Court, feeling utterly miserable.

Then the four other boys were dealt with too. Patrick had a very bad school report and had been in trouble before. So had Fred. The magistrate was very stern with them indeed.

'You will both be sent away to schools for three years,' he said. 'And you will have to stop there the whole of that time if you don't behave yourselves. You were given a chance before, and you haven't taken it. Now you must learn your lesson the hard way.'

He was gentler with poor, frightened Len. 'I think you were under the influence of your big brother,' he told the boy. 'We are going to send you to a nice home, with good people who will love you and teach you many things you haven't learnt. We may let your mother have you back later if she keeps the promise she has made to make a good home for you herself.'

That left only Jack. He was crying. 'Don't send me away, sir,' he begged. 'I'd miss my brothers and sisters, and my Mum.'

'No, don't send him away, sir,' begged Mrs Harris. ' 'Tisn't his fault all this – what can you do when you've got a family of eight and only two small rooms to live in, sir? Do you wonder the boy slips out and stays out and gets into trouble? He's a good boy really, sir.'

'Well, he *hasn't* been a good boy,' said the magistrate. 'And he knows it. Now listen, Mrs Harris – we are going to place him on probation for two years. That means that you and he will have the help of a Probation Officer during that time. She will help you find a bigger place for you and your family to live in. She will also tell us how Jack is behaving.'

'I'll do my best to help him, sir,' said Mrs Harris, earnestly.

'Now, if Jack does well during the next two years, nothing more will be heard of this,' said the magistrate. 'But if the Probation Officer is not satisfied with his conduct, he will have to come here again, and he will then be punished for what he has now done. And, Mrs Harris, I am sure you will see that it is only fair and just that he should pay out of his pocket-money the £5 which is his share of what was stolen.'

'Oh yes, sir,' said Mrs Harris, thankful that Jack was not to be sent away from her.

There was no more to be said. The case was finished. The usher looked up the names of the next children to be called, and the six boys went soberly out with their parents. Bob didn't walk with his mother. He went out some way behind her, looking lonely and frightened.

What was going to happen to him now?

## CHAPTER TWENTY - TWO

## 'Save Me Somehow'

When the Mackenzies heard what had been decided about Bob they were very upset indeed. Why, Bob hadn't even been able to go back to their home and say good-bye! He was to go somewhere for the night before being sent away to the west country to his new foster-home, wherever it was.

He was taken away from the Court by the kindly Probation Officer. He pulled at her arm. 'I don't want to go away,' he said. 'I'll never see my friends the Mackenzies again. I'll never see Pat.'

'I'm afraid you must come along with me,' said the Probation Officer. 'Perhaps your friends will go and see you one day when you have settled down in your new home.'

So Bob went with her. His mother didn't say good-bye to him. Perhaps one day she would wish she had. Perhaps one day she would be lonely and want her son, and he wouldn't be there.

Only Patrick was defiant now. Tom was trying to be brave, saying good-bye to his parents. He was to go off straight away to the Approved School. His mother clung to him, forgetting that she was ashamed of him, remembering only that he was her boy and was going away for a long time.

'We'll have you back in a few months' time, Tom, we will, we will,' she said. 'You'll want to come back, won't you, Tom?'

'I'm standing by you, son,' said his father. 'You'll

always have me at your back in future. Home will be different when you come back.'

Tom's lips trembled. His surliness vanished. Now that he was to be sent away from it home began to seem a most desirable place. He hugged his father and mother, unable to say a single word. Then he had to go, because he was to catch a train that afternoon.

Jeanie, Donald and Pat tore home from school that morning to see if their parents had heard any news of Bob. Their hearts sank when they saw their sober, serious faces.

'What happened to Bob? Where is he?' asked Jeanie. 'Have you heard anything, Mummy? What's happened? Tell us!'

'I'll tell you all I've heard,' said her mother. 'Then, like us, you'll know what happens to children when they go wrong. We've heard about all the six boys – and oh, I'm glad *we've* got good children!'

'I got my sums wrong this morning,' said Pat dismally. 'I wasn't very good.'

Her mother smiled. 'That's not what I was meaning, Pat,' she said.

The three children listened intently to their parents' description of a Juvenile Court and what happens there. Pat began to cry when she heard that Bob was to go away the very next day. She pulled at her father's arm.

'Go and get him,' she begged. 'Go and get him away. Why can't *we* have him? If somebody's got to look after him, why can't *we*? I want Bob. He's my big brother.'

'He's not,' said Donald, jealously. 'I'm your brother.'

'No. You're Jeanie's,' said Pat. 'Bob *said* he would be my brother. Daddy, go and get him.'

'It's not as easy as that, Pat darling,' said her mother, getting up. 'Now really I must go and see to your dinner. Dear, dear – I'll be neglecting *you* next!'

'You won't!' said Donald. 'We won't let you. You couldn't, anyway.'

'Pat, you come out with me and give Frisky his bone,' said Mrs Mackenzie, seeing that Pat was really upset about her news. 'He can't *think* why we are all late for dinner today! He's really looking very worried.'

That evening Pat lay awake a long time. She thought about Bob. How could anyone think he was bad? He wasn't. She knew quite well he wasn't. She wondered what he was doing. Was he asleep or was he wide awake and worried? He hadn't been able to come and say good-bye to her. Pat was sure he would worry about that.

Bob *was* wide awake. It was dark, and he was in a strange place. He missed the Mackenzies. He missed Frisky's cheerful barking. He felt lonely and strange.

He had washed and cleaned his teeth and brushed his hair. He had said his prayers, though he didn't think that God could really care very much about him.

'Don't let me be sent away,' he suddenly prayed in a panic. 'Save me somehow! You know I'm truly truly sorry, please, God. Please, please save me!'

The morning came. He got up and dressed. He had breakfast in a daze, and was then sent to help pile up logs in the garden of the place he was in, with two other boys. It was a Remand Home, and Bob was to be there only one night before he left.

'Your train goes at eleven o'clock,' he was told. 'Someone will fetch you when it's time.'

Ten o'clock came. Half-past ten. Bob's heart sank down into his boots. He had been hoping that Mrs Mackenzie might somehow manage to bring Pat to say good-bye to him.

He heard his name called. 'Robert Kent! Come along in, will you?'

'Time for your train,' said one of the other boys with him. 'Good luck, mate!'

He went in slowly. Nothing could save him now. In ten minutes' time he would be in the train, taken away for good!

'In here, Robert!' called the voice, and Bob walked into a bare little room where visitors were received.

Mr and Mrs Mackenzie were there! Bob looked at them in joy. But they hadn't brought Pat — what a disappointment.

The man in charge of the Remand Home spoke to Bob. 'Robert, I have some news for you. These two friends of yours have been to see various people this morning, including the Probation Officer, to find out if *they* could have you instead of the people at the home we were sending you to — and it has been agreed that you may live with them. That is, if you would like to.'

Bob stared in bewilderment. It was all so sudden that he really couldn't take it in. Then he suddenly realized what it meant.

'Bob, it means you don't have to go away from us, or from your school and your friends,' said Mrs Mackenzie, beaming at him. 'You can come back home with us!'

'*Can* I?' said Bob, staring. 'Oh — is it really true?' It's what I'd like more than anything in the world!'

'It's quite true,' said Mr Mackenzie. 'You know that we believe in you, Bob, so we're willing to have you in our family and look after you. Pat will love to have you — so will Jeanie and Donald.'

Bob took Mrs Mackenzie's hand in both of his. He pressed it against his cheek, hardly able to speak.

'Thank you,' he managed to say. 'I love you.'

'Can he come along straight away?' asked Mr

Mackenzie, turning to the man near by. 'It's all fixed up properly, except for a few details.'

'Yes, Mr Mackenzie. That's quite all right,' said the man. 'A very fine action of yours, if I may say so. Pity more people don't think as you do. Well, Bob – you can go home with your friends. And don't let me ever see you back here again!'

'You never will,' said Bob, and shook the hand held out to him. Then, hardly able to believe in his good luck, he went into the hall and down the steps into the street with the Mackenzies.

'I've been saved after all!' he thought joyfully. 'I must tell Pat all about that. I shall be able to play with her and Jeanie and Donald this evening. I shall sleep in my own bed at Barlings Cottage again. I shall have Frisky coming in to wake me each morning. Oh, I'm *happy*!'

Jeanie, Donald and Pat were amazed and thrilled to see Bob when they got home to dinner that morning. Pat yelled and flung herself on him. Donald slapped him on the back, and Jeanie capered round madly.

'He's come back! He's come back!'

'It's like a fairy-tale!' said Pat, when she heard what had happened. 'Oh, Mummy – you *will* have a big family to look after now – will you be able to manage us?'

'Well, if I can't, Daddy will!' said her mother, ladling out plates of hot stew. 'And if I know anything about Bob he's going to be a great help to me and Daddy.'

'I am,' said Bob. 'I'm going to show you that you've got another son, a big strong one, who'll never say no, whatever you ask him to do. And Jeanie, Donald and Pat have got a brother who'll always stand by them.'

'But you're *my* brother really, more than Jeanie's or Donald's,' said Pat at once. 'They've got each other.'

'Yes – and so have we, Pat,' said Bob, smiling at the delighted little girl. 'Two and two is better than two and one, isn't it?'

'Wuff,' said Frisky, pawing at Bob vigorously. 'Wuff.'

'He says he doesn't want to be left out,' said Pat. 'He says he wants a friend too. Mummy, couldn't we buy another dog so that Frisky isn't lonely?'

'No,' said her mother, firmly. 'If Frisky is lonely, it's his own fault. There are six people in this house always making a fuss of him. Do you hear that Frisky?'

'Wuff!' said Frisky, and lay on his back, pedalling his feet in the air.

Bob laughed. This was home. This was the kind of place he loved!

### CHAPTER TWENTY-THREE

## *One Year Later*

And now, nearly a year later, Bob was going Christmas shopping with Pat. They had both saved up their money and were spending it together on presents for the family. Jeanie and Donald had gone shopping together on their own, as they always did.

Bob had grown and looked big and happy. Pat had grown too, but she was still small, though she had not long since had her ninth birthday party. She hung on to Bob's arm as they went.

'You've been living with us almost a year, Bob,' she said. 'I can't *imagine* living without you in the same house now. You really are one of the family, aren't you?'

'Yes,' said Bob. 'And I can't imagine what it was like living at Hawthorns now! It didn't take my mother long to sell the house and go, did it? Now there's another family there with two children, and Hawthorns isn't a bit the same.'

'Are you going to buy your mother a Christmas present, Bob?' Pat asked.

'Yes I am,' said Bob. 'I used to think horrid things of her, but I don't now. I suppose it's because I've got a family again that I don't mind any more. I do love your mother – she's a *real proper* mother – and I'm glad she lets me call her Auntie Jess. Auntie Jess and Uncle Andy – it's the next best thing to being able to call them Daddy and Mummy, as you do! When I grow up I'm going to make them proud of me.'

'They're proud of you now,' said Pat, skipping as she went. 'So am I. I couldn't do without you now, Bob.'

'Look, there's a red cyclamen plant,' said Bob. 'I gave your mother one last year – but it wasn't bought with my own money. I'm going to buy her that plant, but with my *own* money this year!'

They had great fun shopping. They saw Jeanie and Donald in the distance, carrying parcels. The twins shouted to Bob and Pat.

'Don't walk home with us! We've got a parcel for you that you musn't see, and it keeps coming undone. Go another way.'

Bob grinned. 'Right!' he called. 'Come on, Pat. We'll walk home down another road. Oh – here comes Frisky. Hallo, Frisky, are you coming with us?'

'Wuff,' said Frisky, behaving exactly like his name. The two children turned the corner and went down the road. They came to where some new houses were being built and Bob stopped suddenly.

'What's the matter?' asked Pat.

'Pat — do you remember that cellar-room I told you about, the one the Six Terrors Gang used?' said Bob. 'Well, it's quite near. Like to see it? Soon it will have new houses built over it, and might be filled in. Shall we just peep and see if it's still there?'

'Oh *yes*,' said Pat. She had never seen the little cellar. Bob had never visited it again, either. He had had a peculiar dread of seeing it again. But somehow, now that he was with Pat, he wanted to visit it and show it to her.

He helped her over the rubble. They came to the place where the tumble-down house had been, and where Bob had gone for shelter the year before. He looked round.

'Yes — the entrance is over there,' he said. 'I'd almost forgotten! And to think I found my way to it every evening in the dark!'

He took Pat to the top of the stone steps. She peered down. 'Oooh — it looks horrid. But let's go down. I want to see your meeting-place.'

They went down the steps. It was dark down there, and smelt damp and musty. Bob felt in his pocket for his torch. Good — he had it with him. He switched it on.

He and Pat looked round the cellar. It was empty now except for an old box. Bob sat down on it, sudden memories filling his mind.

'This is where we met,' he said to Pat. 'We had an oil stove to warm it — and candles to light it. We made it very cosy, Pat. And Fred had a telephone.'

'A *telephone*!' said Pat, amazed. 'Where?'

'It was only a toy one,' said Bob, remembering the wonderful telephone calls Fred used to make to his imaginary 'men'. 'Look, I used to sit here — this was my corner. And Fred and Tom there; and Len in that corner, and Jack and Patrick here. It was a bit crowded, but we all loved this place then.'

'I can't think why you did!' said Pat, shivering. 'I wonder where everyone will be this Christmas – all the six boys. I know where *you* will be, anyway!'

'Yes – sitting at your Christmas table,' said Bob. 'With a father and mother and you and Jeanie and Donald. I belong to a family now. But what about the others – the other five of the Six Terrors? Where will they be?' Yes, where would they be? Where were they now, and what had happened to them? Bob sat and remembered them all.

Tom now – what was Tom doing? Ah, Tom was coming home for Christmas! Tom had made good at the Approved School, and had earned high praise from the Headmaster. Tom had found that it was simply dreadful having to leave his home and not go back for months and months on end. He missed his sisters and his parents terribly, and had been miserably home-sick.

154

And his family had missed Tom. They remembered his good ways and not his bad ones, they thought of his jokes and not of his tempers. Tom's punishment had been as much of a lesson to his family as to him.

Tom was going back home for good, and he could hardly wait for the day. His sisters had written to him often. He could tell from their letters that things were much, much better at home. He counted the weeks to his return, then the days – and at last the hours.

'We've all got another chance now,' his father said. 'And we must all take it. "One for all and all for one" must be our motto in future.'

And Patrick? No, there was not good news of Patrick. He was cunning and deceitful, and he still told lies. What was going to happen to him in the future? Nobody could tell. He might learn to be honest and to go straight – or it might be too late. It depended on Patrick himself. So far his Headmaster was displeased with him, and there was no chance of Patrick's going free.

Len was back with his mother, happy and behaving himself. His mother would never be a good one, but at least she tried better with Len. Fred was still away, and would be for a long time. He too had a great deal to learn.

Jack was at home, of course still on probation, seeing the Probation Officer regularly, and trying to do his best. But now his home was very different from the one he had had last Christmas!

He told Len all about it when he met him. 'We've got a new house, Len,' he said, jubilantly. 'A much bigger one. Me and Alan sleep in a room together all alone, instead of sharing with all the others! And we've got a tiny garden. Coo – I shan't be bad again, now I've got a proper home!'

Bob thought of the old Six Terrors Gang, as he sat

down in the cellar with little Pat. He wondered if any of the gang were thinking of him too. His eyes roamed round the tiny place.

'Look, Pat!' he said, 'there's a stump of candle left on that ledge! I lit that on Christmas Day last year. And look – there's a bit of coloured paper left in that corner. That must have been a piece of the decorations. We decorated the cellar beautifully.'

Pat picked up the bit of paper. Under it was something else – a tiny parcel wrapped in faded red paper.

'What's this?' she asked.

Bob took it. 'Why – it's one of the presents I put on the little tree I got ready for the boys,' he said. 'It must have fallen off when the police took the tree away. It's a present I got for Tom.'

'Undo it,' said Pat. So Bob undid it, and inside was a rubber, like the ones they had at school, but bigger. 'That's what I got for Tom,' said Bob.

Pat took it and began to rub the cellar-floor with it.

'What are you doing that for?' said Bob.

Pat looked at him solemnly. 'I'm rubbing out that dreadful time you had when you lived down here!' she said. 'I'm rubbing out all the nastiness and horridness and miserableness. Can't you feel it going, because I'm rubbing it away?'

Bob laughed. 'You do such funny things, Pat,' he said. 'But you don't need to do any rubbing, because the nastiness is all gone now. It seems like a dream. Come along – let's go home. It's cold here.'

He took a last look round as he went. Soon a new house would be built over the cellar. What a horrid ugly place it seemed now – but how beautiful it had looked to him that last Christmas Day! He remembered the little candles on the Christmas tree, and the warm glow of the oil stove. He had tried so hard to make some sort of home because he hadn't got a proper one.

But now he had. He forgot his memories and ran up the steps after Pat. Frisky was waiting for them at the top, looking impatient. Frisky didn't like dark damp cellars, and he couldn't inagine why they had gone down there. He jumped up at them, barking, his tail wagging vigorously.

'Good old Frisky,' said Bob, patting him. 'Come along home. It's getting dark.'

Frisky trotted in front, his tail waving. Pat and Bob hurried back to Barlings Cottage. Bob saw that the curtains were drawn across, but that a little crack was left, through which the light shone brightly.

'Pat,' he said. 'Go in first, and take Frisky. I want to do something I used to do, and see what it feels like. Go on in!'

Pat ran in, puzzled; but she always did what Bob said. Frisky ran with her.

Bob crept into the garden and went up to the window. He looked through the crack in the curtains as he had done several times the year before. He saw Mrs Mackenzie getting tea, with Jeanie at the fire, toasting bread. He saw Donald showing his mother something he had bought.

Then in ran Pat and her mother ruffled her hair and kissed her. Frisky leapt about, barking as usual, telling the family he was pleased to be back. Mr Mackenzie wasn't home yet – but Bob saw his pipe-rack, his slippers and his armchair ready for him.

'I used to envy them because I hadn't a family too,' he thought. 'But now it's *my* family. I don't need to peep. I belong! Here I go walking in, to join my family!'

And he went in with his parcels, smiling all over

his face. He didn't need to peep through curtains any more!

Goodbye, Bob, and good luck. You've got what you wanted and you'll hold on to it. Goodbye to all the Six Terrors. What will happen to them in the future? Nobody knows yet – that's quite another story!

# ENID BLYTON

If you're an eager Beaver reader, perhaps you ought to try some more of our exciting Enid Blyton titles. They are available in bookshops or they can be ordered directly from us. Just complete the form below, enclose the right amount of money and the books will be sent to you at home.

| | |
|---|---|
| ☐ Bimbo and Topsy | 85p |
| ☐ The Wishing-Chair Again | £1.75 |
| ☐ Hello, Mr Twiddle! | 85p |
| ☐ Well, Really, Mr Twiddle! | 90p |
| ☐ The Magic Faraway Tree | £1.75 |
| ☐ The Folk of the Faraway Tree | £1.75 |
| ☐ Up the Faraway Tree | £1.50 |
| ☐ The Enchanted Wood | £1.50 |
| ☐ Hollow Tree House | £1.75 |
| ☐ The Adventurous Four | £1.50 |
| ☐ The Adventurous Four Again | £1.50 |
| ☐ The Naughtiest Girl is a Monitor | £1.95 |
| ☐ The Naughtiest Girl in the School | £1.95 |

If you would like to order books, please send this form, and the money due to:

ARROW BOOKS, BOOKSERVICE BY POST, PO BOX 29, DOUGLAS, ISLE OF MAN, BRITISH ISLES. Please enclose a cheque or postal order made out to Arrow Books Ltd for the amount due including 30p per book for postage and packing both for orders within the UK and for overseas orders.

NAME ...............................................

ADDRESS ...........................................

......................................................

*Please print clearly.*